HER BABY'S
SECRET FATHER

I'd like to dedicate this book to my fabulous
critique partners: Roben, Thieme, Gina,
Deanne, and Trish.
Ladies, you're the best.

CHAPTER ONE

THE nurses gathered around the huge panoramic window like they always did at six-thirty each Monday morning. For a moment they'd put aside any last-minute shift-change bustle or patient-charting to enjoy what nature offered. Excited, expectant, they gabbed and giggled while their eyes fixed on the Chinese elm-lined streets that led to the back of Mercy Hospital in northeast Los Angeles.

Jaynie Winchester didn't approve of their gawking, but who was she to tell them to stop? As charge nurse for the small pulmonary ward, she knew when to crack the whip and when to let her co-workers enjoy a moment's reprieve from their hectic schedules. She'd studied the statistics and knew mutual respect boosted morale on any difficult hospital ward. And their heavily burdened floor catered to ventilator patients and every imaginable respiratory ailment. Bottom line, the nurses deserved their thirty-second fantasy break.

Any other day she'd pretend to be preoccupied with nursing duties while the scrub-clad ladies gaped—and from the corner of her eye watch right along with them.

Today, though, she was distracted with annoying, moderately painful Braxton Hicks cramping. False labor. What else could you call it at less than seven months gestation? She'd felt so energetic on Sunday. Perhaps she'd overdone it, stenciling the butter-yellow nursery walls with plump, fuzzy ducklings wearing cute blue bonnets and vests.

Jaynie blamed the Mexican food she'd eaten for dinner as the cause of her little one's spurt of activity throughout the night. The baby had rolled and tumbled, she'd cramped on and off, and because of it had gotten little sleep.

A sudden rise in the nurses' chatter, followed

by awestruck silence, alerted Jaynie that the moment they'd been waiting for had arrived. She rubbed her abdomen, adjusted her small, wire-framed glasses, and wandered toward the early-morning light that poured through the huge window. Heck, she deserved a treat too.

Without fail, at six-thirty, sinewy Terrance Zanderson jogged up the sidewalk, his scant shorts revealing magnificent masculine legs. With thigh muscles tight and bulging, he ran like an Olympic gold medallist. His long, tanned torso met with the nurses' overwhelming approval, if their sighs were any indication. Taut abdominal muscles could be seen even from the second story distance. Strong, shapely deltoids rippled with each swing of his arm.

A pleasant memory came to mind of the month she'd actually dated Terrance last year. She'd been well set on her plans for motherhood by then, and hadn't wanted anything to get in the way. And besides, his life had been way too hectic, with his pursuit of medical school while being the day supervisor of the

Respiratory Therapy Department, and all his sports activities on top of that. After her last disastrous relationship, she'd expected more from a man than he'd been ready or able to give, and they'd parted amicably.

Aside from being a work of art, what moved Jaynie the most was Terrance's flowing auburn-colored hair that barely kissed his shoulders. A shade or two lighter and he would nearly be a redhead, a personal favorite of hers. The clean-shaven, chiseled face, square jaw and predominant nose weren't half bad either. She tamped down a warm, visceral response in her gut.

Why hadn't she slept with him when she'd had the chance?

The man never let the nurses down. Just before he moved out of their sight and into the ER entrance of the hospital, he lifted a flaw-lessly sculpted arm and waved. The shameless, worshipful gaggle of pulmonary nurses erupted with squeals and giggles as they waved back. They didn't care that he'd caught them gawking—again. Getting an eyeful of Terrance was worth the embarrassment.

Jaynie smiled.

"Back to work, ladies. Show's over," she said, straightening and smoothing her uniform maternity smock.

A long group sigh followed, then the women dispersed for one last cup of institution coffee prior to taking report for the day.

After completing the change-of-shift narcotics count, Jaynie hurried to the nursing lounge for a visit to the bathroom before beginning her day. Kim Lee scurried in on a breeze of fresh herbal shampoo, arriving a millisecond before the night shift reported off.

"What did you do to your hair?" Jaynie stood in mid-yawn with belly extended, hands resting at kidney level.

"I had it straightened," Kim said.

"But you already have straight hair."

Jaynie gaped at the board-straight, waist-length black tresses with electric blue chemically woven highlights. She thought about her own unruly brown curls that she battled each morning, most often settling for drawing them tightly back into an exploding ponytail. Her hand grazed her face; as usual, a few renegade ringlets had escaped.

Kim scooped her hair over her shoulder and began a quick braid with nimble fingers. "All the Asian girls are doing it." When she'd finished, she twisted the hair into a bun and draped her fuchsia-colored stethoscope around her neck.

"If you say so."

Jaynie took a quick breath and blew slowly between pursed lips. Another Braxton Hicks cramp grabbed her attention and held it for several seconds. She checked her watch. Only five minutes since the last one had occurred. Odd. She rubbed her hands around her bulging tummy as if it were a genie's bottle, and ignored her discomfort by talking to her friend.

"So, how was your date with the pharmacist last night?"

Kim's black almond-shaped eyes sparkled with delight. "Szechwan-hot, baby."

Jaynie blurted a laugh, but when a sharp pain struck like lightning, she grabbed her friend's arm. "Ouch!" It built… "Ouch, ouch!" …into a bona fide contraction.

Kim clutched Jaynie's shoulders. "What's wrong?"

Gasping, a typhoon of fear broke over her as water splattered down her legs onto the linoleum floor. "It's too soon!"

Kim jumped to action, shouting commands. "Call Labor and Delivery," she yelled to one of the nurses through the door, "Tell them we're coming." She rushed back to Jaynie's side. "Where's our wheelchair?" Panic punctuated each word. "I'm a pulmonary nurse," the lithe R.N. emphasized as she scurried to the linen closet across the hall and grabbed a towel. "I don't know anything about birthing babies."

Jaynie longed to reassure her friend, but instead became distracted with increasing pain, and decided to work at reassuring herself.

I've read dozens of books. I can do this.

A wheelchair appeared from nowhere, and

someone shoved it behind Jaynie's knees. With the help of no less than six other hands, she eased herself down onto the plastic blue absorbent pad haphazardly placed on the seat.

"Don't forget to breathe, Jaynie." The calm voice of reason from an older nurse, who'd had several children, comforted her.

Piece of cake. Right.

"Who-who-who, *heeeeee.*" She diligently repeated the 4/4 breathing rhythm she'd read about.

Kim popped a wheelie with the chair, avoiding the puddle on the floor, and raced toward the white-brick-walled corridor.

"Someone call Housekeeping!" Jaynie called over her shoulder, and pointed toward the mess. "I mean Environmental Services. So no one will slip and fall."

"Don't you dare have the baby in the elevator!" Kim's eyes had doubled in size.

"How can I?" Jaynie said between breaths. "I haven't gone to Lamaze classes yet!" A second wave of pain clued her in to the realization that she was in labor. "Something tells me I don't have much control…"

For the first time in ages, Jaynie had to give in to a power much greater than her self-determination. Labor. Every aspect of her pregnancy had been plotted to a tee…but this. Nope, controlling the birth of her baby was definitely beyond her will of steel.

The obstetric nurses were ready the minute Jaynie rolled through the automatic doors.

"Hey, Nurse Winchester, what's happ'nin'?" A friendly voice and smile from Latasha Hobbs greeted her. "Put her there," she said to Kim, pointing to Room C on the Labor/Delivery/Recovery Ward. "We'll take over from here."

Kim followed the nurse's order.

Quicker than Jaynie could say "Ouch!" the tall, lean woman removed her from the wheelchair, had her positioned on the bed, and checked her blood pressure and pulse. "You don't look so big. How far along are you, hun?"

"Not quite twenty-eight weeks."

Latasha scrunched her nose. "Kinda early.

We better get an order for Terbutaline to ward off labor."

Kim gave a reassuring grasp to Jaynie's shoulder and whispered, "You're going to be fine."

"I know." She faked a confident smile. "You go back to Pulmonary before they start paging you, okay?"

After squeezing her arm one last time, Kim hesitated, but left the bedside. She paused again at the door with a concerned look, and gave a delicate wave before disappearing. Jaynie hid her fear and waved back.

Another nurse, with broad shoulders, magenta-colored spiky hair, and a "been there, done that" confidence, appeared with an intravenous tray.

"You're in luck," Latasha said. "It's slow today, so Nurse Martin is going to help out."

"I'm Gail. I'll start the IV," the large woman said.

"Did your water break?" Latasha furrowed her brow the slightest bit.

"Just now, on the Pulmonary Ward."

"Let me help you get undressed, Ms Mother-to-be." Latasha spoke with a friendly voice that gave Jaynie a sense of comfort. She reached for Jaynie's scrub top and removed it in record time. A pro at patient admission, with the intake sheet memorized, the nurse asked the necessary questions while assisting Jaynie. "Okay, Mommy, off with the bra and pants."

Together, between contractions, they removed the soaked scrub pants and then her bra. Jaynie was normally modest, but the shock of being stripped naked in front of total strangers took a backseat to the more pressing business at hand. Labor!

Latasha threw an extra-large hospital gown over Jaynie. She moved efficiently and placed a long elastic strap behind her back, fastening it on top of her stomach. Jaynie jumped when the nurse squirted a cold glob of lubrication jelly onto her skin. Latasha positioned a fetal heart-rate dopler over the best spot, creating an immediate muffled, rhythmic thump-swish, thump-swish sound. The contraction-measuring device was placed snugly over the firmest portion of her abdomen.

"Here comes another one." Latasha's attention darted to the bedside machine graphing the movement of the contraction. The baby's pulse accelerated with the mounting pressure from the tightened uterus. The graph looked like a small peaked mountain, and just above it danced the ragged pattern of the baby's heart-rate, ranging from 140 to 160 beats per minute.

Latasha announced, "Looks like a healthy baby!" and smiled reassuringly at her—until she checked her temperature. "Low grade," she commented. "Are you allergic to any antibiotics?"

"No," Jaynie answered.

Gail went to work with a tourniquet and an intravenous catheter on Jaynie's right arm.

"I've got better veins on the left side." Ever the patient advocate, Jaynie spoke up for herself in mid-contraction. "Who-who-who, *heeee*."

"Always listen to the patient when it comes to veins," Latasha reminded the other nurse. "You'd better draw some labs, while you're at it. Forget the Terbutaline; looks like we're going to labor her out."

Gail screwed up her mouth, but undid the tourniquet and moved to the other side of the bed. Latasha gloved up and took a peek under Jaynie's gown.

"The amniotic fluid looks clear, no sign of meconium. I'm going to take a group beta strep culture while I'm in the neighborhood. Are you registered here at Mercy Hospital for delivery?" she asked, while she swiped her perineum with a long cotton-tipped swab.

"Nope. I was planning on delivering at home with a midwife." Jaynie felt a cold hand get up close and personal. She gasped, and thought that after all of the prenatal appointments she'd had, she should be used to it by now.

Latasha's excited velvet-black eyes met Jaynie's. "Get a move on, Gail, she's completely effaced and—" she held up the three gloved fingers she'd used to measure the distance "—five centimeters dilated. Let's have us a baby."

Another contraction, only three minutes since the last, grabbed Jaynie's undivided attention.

Gail pierced her skin with the intravenous needle. Jaynie gasped again. Small lab vials were quickly filled with blood.

"Make sure to get a type and crossmatch," Latasha said to Gail. Glancing at Jaynie, she asked, "You want me to call the father?"

"There is no father," Jaynie managed to say while concentrating on her breathing. She glimpsed the telling look in the nurses' eyes.

Like everyone else, they'd jumped to conclusions. Well, it wasn't like that for her. She hadn't got knocked up and left behind. She'd walked away from her boyfriend of five years when she'd finally realized all he ever wanted was a lifetime girlfriend, never a wife. Two years ago she'd realized she wanted a family, and last year, at the age of thirty-four, had started making a plan on her own.

A two-part plan. The first part, to pad her bank account by working like a madwoman; the second, to waste no more time gambling on finding the right guy. She'd then meticulously researched sperm banks for the best possible gene pool, and that was what had led her to Mercy Hospital in Los Angeles: a world-class sperm bank at the medical university a short distance away.

There had been just one problem, though. She'd met, and become immediately attracted to, Terrance Zanderson. He'd definitely had possibilities, but something dark and deep in his eyes had alerted Jaynie that he'd never commit. And his schedule had been a killer. She hadn't been able to compete with prerequisites for med school, or his avid love of rock climbing and extreme sports.

She was well aware that hospital gossip implicated him as the baby's father. Let them think what they may. Her lips were sealed.

* * *

Swept up by the mounting pain, Jaynie only remembered bits and pieces from the frantic moments—or was it hours?—that followed. Gail hung a small piggyback bottle of antibiotics along with the intravenous fluid; a precaution since Jaynie's water had broken and she had a low-grade temperature. Latasha scurried around preparing for the imminent birth, assembling basins and various clamps. In between, like a good nurse, she held Jaynie's hand at the apex of her contractions, and periodically checked and measured her progress.

Since she'd insisted on natural childbirth, mostly what Jaynie remembered was pain. Pain taking control of her body as she'd never felt before. Pain strong enough that she imagined her neck lengthening and her head spinning around three times like the girl in *The Exorcist*. Pain excruciating enough to take her over the edge and have her spewing undignified words and insults at the L & D nurses. Finally, when she thought she couldn't bear another second of it, a wave of relief rolled along and replaced the pain with an overwhelming urge to push.

Together, the nurses switched the labor bed into a delivery table just before the obstetrician entered the birthing suite. The masked, goggled and gowned on-call M.D. briefly introduced himself. Jaynie nodded a beleaguered greeting, and went back to work, pushing so hard she feared she might develop an aneurysm.

She overheard the word "crowning", and then, "The heart-rate is decelerating too low. The cord must be in the way." And, "It's too late for a C-section." And "We haven't got time to call the NICU team, the baby's here."

Jaynie screamed with one last mega-push and felt a tremendous rush of relief when her baby's head was delivered. One more push and the body came out.

Someone said, "It's a girl."

And then silence.

She struggled to raise her head, and glimpsed her tiny, opaque-pale baby in the lap of the obstetrician, floppy and inanimate. She panicked.

"Cry, sweetie. Come on, cry," she urged.

One last beat of silence before the doctor clamped and snipped the umbilical cord. He handed the baby to Latasha, who placed her on the warming table to suction her mouth and nose, and to stimulate her skin with vigorous rubbing.

From the corner of her eye, Jaynie saw the doctor walk to the intercom and press it with his elbow. "Code Pink, Delivery Room C. Code Pink."

She recognized the Mercy Hospital term for newborn distress, and prayed a quiet, frantic prayer that the code team would respond quickly.

"Cry, my Tara. Cry," she pleaded.

Terrance had showered and changed into his working scrubs. He'd taken an end-of-shift report from the night respiratory supervisor, given work assignments to the other therapists, and had made it halfway through ventilator rounds by mid-morning.

The pulmonary floor bustled with excitement over their charge nurse's surprise labor. He couldn't help overhearing Kim Lee retell several of the nurses the whole story about Jaynie.

A twinge of sadness niggled at his brain. Maybe because he knew he could never give Jaynie what she wanted more than anything in the world—a child. And she'd moved on alone with her life while he was still chipping away at his plans to get accepted to med school. He didn't believe in melancholy, so he punted the thought right out of his mind and got back to work.

Once he'd completed his rounds, he decided to go to the Neonatal Intensive Care Unit, which happened to be close to where Jaynie was. He'd use the excuse of relieving the NICU respiratory therapist for a lunchbreak. Eleven-thirty a.m. was almost lunchtime, right? That way he could keep tabs on how her delivery was going.

He remembered seeing Jaynie for the first time a little over a year ago at a new employee orientation. As the supervisor, he'd been called on to give a brief welcoming speech about the Respiratory Therapy department to the most recently hired group.

His mind had gone blank when he'd seen the wild-haired brunette with bright brown eyes, smiling and staring expectantly at him through tiny wire glasses. Most people might have thought she looked plain, but not him. The opposite of California-superficial, she was natural and appealing as all hell. Her generous lips had made him wonder how soft they might be to kiss, and every bit of the information he'd meant to impart about the benefits of working for Mercy Hospital had slipped out of his head.

He smiled ruefully. He'd since found out how it felt to kiss her. *Astounding*. And she still had a way of emptying his mind of all other thoughts. But none of it mattered. Things hadn't worked out between them.

Within two minutes of his taking over the other R.T.'s workload, the Code Pink alert crackled over the NICU intercom.

A shot of adrenaline and a surge of fear caused a knee-jerk reflex. He stopped what he was doing and raced toward the Labor and Delivery suite, heart pounding in his chest, practically bowling over the diminutive neonatologist in the hall.

The doctor had handed the limp newborn to Latasha instead of placing the baby on Jaynie's tummy for immediate bonding. She raised her head again. The midwife she'd planned on having had promised she'd get to hold her baby right after delivery. Latasha suctioned the baby's nose and mouth and rubbed away some vernix caseosa—the white material that gave the fetus protection while floating in the amniotic fluid of the uterus.

Two people burst into the room. Terrance eclipsed a small Indian man, Dr. Shrinivasan. Jaynie trusted Terrance's skill as a respiratory therapist, and knew the doctor was a particularly talented neonatologist. Seeing both of them rush in to save the day made her feel hopeful that all would turn out well.

The obstetrician spoke quietly to the neonatologist. The APGARS at one and five minutes—the five objective signs evaluating the newborn's condition: heart-rate, respiratory effort, muscle tone, reflex irritability and color—were anything but impressive. Her baby girl needed emergency assistance with her breathing.

Latasha came back and stayed by Jaynie's side, assisting with the afterbirth. Jaynie watched the baby-warmer like a mother hawk circling a nest.

It had only taken a few compressions on the Ambu-Bag before her preemie was able to take some breaths on her own. But she'd been inconsistent, so Terrance had slid a tiny airway down her throat and continued using the small bellows bag to blow air fortified with extra oxygen into her premature lungs.

He and the doctor rolled the whole unit out of the room toward Neonatal Intensive Care, where a ventilator awaited.

Jaynie's plans and dreams careened out the

door to another place—a world she had no control of. She watched helplessly, and prayed.

Please, God, don't take my baby.

CHAPTER TWO

TERRANCE knew the story well from his experience in the NICU. Though viable outside the womb, this baby was over eight weeks premature. Her lungs weren't ready for life in the big, bad, smog-ridden Los Angeles basin.

He squinted and pinched his nose as nightmarish thoughts appeared about the loss of his own child to crib death six years ago. He shook his head and tried to force the vision of his baby girl out of his mind. He'd never forget her beautiful little face, not as long as he lived.

When he hadn't been able to save his own daughter, he'd vowed to become a respiratory therapist. But now, several years later, that wasn't enough. He wanted to be a pediatrician. Regardless of what he'd have to sacrifice in his personal life, he'd see to it that he made it to his dream.

Jaynie's premature baby had pinked up beautifully after intubation. The report from the NICU doc had been a good one. No meconium or amniotic fluid had gotten into the little one's lungs. The oxygen saturation in her blood was holding at ninety-two percent or greater on the ventilator, and if all went well she'd be downgraded to backup assist control breathing, and then extubated in a few days.

As he adjusted the ventilator settings, he noted that many of the typical newborn reflexes were intact: the startle reflex, the grasp reflex and, his personal favorite, the tonic neck reflex. He got a kick out of how it looked like a fencing position. Lying on her back, the baby turned her head to the left, extending the arm and leg on the same side, and flexed the opposite arm and leg.

On guard!

"Hey, Peanut," he said, reaching onto the open radiant warmer that gave all the NICU personnel easy access to a preemie. He gently patted the scrawny, barely three-pound newborn's head. The baby was startled, but couldn't utter a peep due to the ventilator. "I'm sorry."

The overhead heater beamed on his hands like a sunlamp, keeping the wee one's temperature stable. "That's right, you go ahead and protest. That's a good sign." Terrance smiled and played with her fingers as he administered a minuscule amount of bronchial medicine through the pulmonary device.

He didn't often assign himself to the NICU, but decided for the next couple of days he'd keep an eye on Jaynie's preemie. *Just until she's out of the woods,* he rationalized. Today, he'd scheduled himself for a second shift until eleven p.m., to keep guard over the newborn's first day. Besides, Mercy Hospital always seemed short on staff from far too many sick leave calls.

With excellent weather almost every day in Southern California, and good employee benefits, many were tempted to play hooky on a regular basis. He figured he'd save the hospital from paying extra for a registry R.T., and he planned to put the overtime salary to good use to help pay for future med school costs.

The Peanut squirmed and jerked her skinny little limbs, and moved her perfect but premature head, and Terrance swore she looked straight at him through puffy, newborn eye-slits.

"Tough trip out, kid? You look like a prize fighter." He tenderly touched the baby's crown with a gloved hand and bet she'd eventually have red hair, if the faintly colored down on her scalp were any indication.

His heart lurched as he remembered his own daughter had had red hair, like his twin sister.

He understood that the less an infant weighed at delivery, the greater was the possibility of crib death. And this baby's low APGARS and respiratory difficulties could increase her risk of SIDS.

He pondered what that meant.

A second wave of memories fought their way

to the surface of his mind. After being trapped by his college girlfriend, who had sworn she was on birth control pills, he had done the honorable thing and married her. He hadn't exactly been thrilled about becoming a father at twenty-three, having just graduated with a liberal arts degree and not having a job. But when his child had been born, he'd immediately fallen in love with her.

His baby had died silently and unexpectedly at four months, from sudden infant death syndrome. It had nearly broken his spirit. Hell, it had hurt him so deeply that he'd vowed never to have another child.

When his wife had started abusing prescription drugs, he'd got her help. But when she'd had an affair, he'd ended the marriage.

He'd become very cynical about love. *No family for me.* In a strange way, that pledge had freed him to pursue his dreams of becoming a doctor so he could help other people's kids.

Terrance played with the little one's hand and discovered himself smiling again when she grasped his finger. It gave him a different kind of rush, warm and precious, and it took him a second to register the foreign feeling. *Oh, no.* He winked at the newborn while gathering his defenses. *I'm not going to fall for that.*

He studied the tiny hand that could barely wrap around his thumb, and thought he'd miscounted. One, two, three, four, five…six? He released it to check the other hand, counted, found the same number.

He glanced up to the knowing look of a nearby elderly NICU nurse. She nodded and whispered, "Polydactyly."

Wasn't that a genetic fluke that ran in families?

"Well, Miss…" He looked at the first name on the layette in the NICU and lifted an eyebrow. "Well, Miss Tara." Terrance thought about the coincidence—the baby had his twin sister's name. "May I call you Peanut?" He adjusted the small blue plastic tubing on the nebulizer portion of the ventilator that delivered medicine to help dilate the bronchial airways of her tiny lungs. "Let's put a positive spin on this. The way I see it, you're an over-achiever already."

Jaynie got out of bed for the first time after delivery and almost fainted. A student nurse appeared from nowhere to sweep an arm around her waist.

"What are you trying to do? Fall flat on your face?" The fresh-faced youngster practically carried her to the bathroom, where she'd been headed. "Didn't we tell you to call for help? Why is it that nurses are always the worst patients?" She shook her head of dark straight hair and grunted, giving Jaynie a look of disgust.

Jaynie shrugged her shoulders and apologized for trying to be self-sufficient. "I thought I was okay."

The nurse-in-training clicked her tongue. "That's what they all say."

She positioned Jaynie safely inside the bathroom, showed her the button to push for help—as if she'd never seen one before—and closed the door.

Her stomach felt empty and sagging. Heavy post-partum lochia dampened her mesh padded panties. A thought about senior citizens wearing similar underwear for bladder control popped into her head. She couldn't wait to change into a fresh pair, and wondered if they might come in a French-cut style. For the first time since becoming a mother, Jaynie smiled at her own corny joke. Heck, maybe there was even a thong version?

The intravenous line of saline and sugar water felt more like a ball and chain. The tall metal pole on wheels carried a volume-regulating machine and was necessary because of her ongoing low-grade fever and her need for anti-biotics.

So this is how my patients feel. It seemed odd, being on the other side of the hospital gowns and curtains.

Her legs trembled with each step, as if she'd just run a marathon. She smelled like she'd run one, too, and dreamed about a soothing warm shower. For now, a birdbath would have to suffice. Oh, but the warm institution-white cotton washcloth felt spectacular on her face. She didn't even mind the harsh laundry detergent smell.

They said her labor had only lasted four hours—four of the longest, most grueling hours of her life. She glanced at the clock on the wall. Five o'clock. She must have passed out for a while afterwards. The last thing she remembered was waiting to hear her baby cry… But she hadn't heard a sound.

Now, holding the washcloth over her eyes, she could almost hear the sound of her baby being whisked away on the combination Infant Warmer-Crash Cart. Wanting to cry, she talked herself out of it. "You've got to be strong for Tara."

After cleaning up, all Jaynie could think about was going to see her baby, the child she'd named Tara Elizabeth Winchester. Elizabeth after her mother, and Tara after a special little girl in a picture provided by the sperm bank.

The children in the photo couldn't have been more than two years old, and must have been related. The girl's wild and curly hair drew attention away from the stoic, straight-haired, cowlick-ridden boy by her side. The black and white Xeroxed copy had made it impossible to tell what color her hair was. Her shirt had a big heart next to her name—Tara. The boy's name, the name of her sperm donor, had been removed for confidentiality. Perhaps the other name had been an oversight? From the looks of it, they were twins.

"You gave us a scare," the obstetric doctor said, appearing at her door.

Jaynie snapped out of her thoughts and turned in the chair by the window. "Oh, Dr. Lindsay. Is everything okay?"

"All is well. Your baby simply made her appearance on the planet too soon," he said. "The neonatologist wants to fatten her up a bit. They'll keep her on a ventilator for a while, then watch to see how she adjusts to breathing on her own." He scrubbed his fatigued-looking face with a large hand—evidence of a long day. "I need to put you back in bed for a moment." He walked closer. "Let me check your fundus. Are you feeling okay?"

She lay down on the hospital bed so the doctor could press on her lower abdomen and her ever-tightening uterus. The nurses had been doing frequent checks, and had told her after the last time that she was the size of a grapefruit.

"Progress," he said. "You should be good to go home by tomorrow."

Tomorrow? The thought of leaving for home without Tara sucked the wind out of Jaynie's lungs.

Shortly after the doctor left, Kim showed up, wearing hip-hugging cropped pants and a bright, silky Mandarin collar top, and pushing a wheelchair. "It's visiting hours. Let's roll to look at Tara. Maybe if I pull a few strings they'll let me in, too."

Down the hall, Kim and Jaynie found the rectangular, sterile NICU room silent and solemn when they entered. Fluorescent light gave the room a false midday look, when it was well past the dinner hour. Ten incubators lined the walls, but only six had occupants. Her baby lay in one, and she couldn't wait to see her. A few parents congregated around other stations, speaking reverently to their preemies.

And there, by the radiant warmer second from the end, much to Jaynie's surprise, stood Terrance Zanderson. He spoke almost inaudibly to her daughter, while giving her a breathing treatment.

The sight of the tall, handsome man, whispering like a father to her baby, squeezed her heart. She blamed post-partum hormones for the sudden blurring of her vision and the catch in her throat. Too bad things hadn't worked out.

If only Tara had a doting father like Terrance to call her own. But that wasn't part of the plan. All the research in the world couldn't produce an in-the-flesh, willing-to-commit parent for her girl.

Feeling much stronger, and eager to see Tara, Jaynie jumped from the wheelchair and approached Terrance and the layette in her hospital-issue, skid-free slipper socks.

"Hey," he said, looking surprised.

"Hey," she whispered, fearing she'd wake not only her baby, but everyone else's if she spoke too loud. "What are you still doing here?"

"I'm doing a double shift," he replied with a smile. "I'm fiendishly making extra dough to fend off future med school costs."

Jaynie nodded. She knew about his big plans. They'd talked for hours on their very first date about their life's plans. At thirty, his had been medical school—though he'd never completely explained why he wanted to make the switch from R.T. to M.D. At thirty-four, hers had been motherhood, and she hadn't given him the full story of why either. She'd seen the terrorized look in his eyes when she'd blatantly come out and told him what she wanted most in life. But he hadn't run away kicking and screaming, like her ex-boyfriend. He'd even asked her out for another date. And another. And another.

Yet, with their divergent plans, there had been no place for their attraction to lead. But they'd ended on a positive note, remaining friends.

The crusty NICU nurse greeted Jaynie with antibacterial soap scrub for her hands, shooed Kim out of the room, and took control of the layette and the baby within. "Has your milk come in yet?" she asked, handing a mask to Jaynie to wear.

Mildly embarrassed in front of Terrance, Jaynie shook her head. She couldn't tear her eyes away from her precious daughter even while she applied the mask.

"We've got an electric pump in the other room. You can plug yourself in and save the colostrum for Tara's feedings. With o2 Sats like hers, I predict she'll be extubated by the end of the week. Right, Terrance?"

He nodded his agreement and smiled warmly at Jaynie—a picture that brightened her spirit.

"She's a fighter," he said. "She'll be fine; don't worry. The respirator is just helping save her energy, by not having to work so hard for each breath."

His comforting words touched her, but Jaynie was no fool. She knew the biggest threat to her preemie was infection, and the next few days could bring disaster or smooth sailing. Only time would tell.

The NICU nurse, garbed in pale green scrubs, blue surgery cap and latex-free gloves, said, "Once she's extubated, we'll have to see if she's got a rooting reflex, so she can nurse."

The R.N. ushered Jaynie alongside the layette. Encumbering ventilator apparatus was connected to the endotracheal tube in Tara's mouth, which passed into her windpipe and made little peeping sounds as it pushed air into her lungs. Cardio-respirator leads were in place on her chest and abdomen, along with a temperature sensor on the other side of her tiny stomach.

Jaynie briefly studied the numbers on the monitors, deciding they were good. Then she noticed Tara's thigh was bound to a board, to secure IV tubing into a large vein, and more tubing was threaded into an umbilical vessel.

The sight of her own flesh and blood lying fragile and helpless on a large sterile-looking box, with overhead lights like Friday-night football, took the air from her lungs. She steadied herself against a moment of dizziness. Touching the thin, birth-wrinkled skin on her baby's side, to make sure she was real, she watched Tara twitch and squirm in response.

The heart-wrenching sight throbbed in Jaynie's chest. She ached for her child. What a rotten way to come into the world…but at least she was alive. She said a silent prayer of thanks to God, and blew out her breath in a rush of emotion.

The tiniest disposable diaper she'd ever imagined gaped at the legs of her scrawny newborn. She couldn't help but shake her head and smile in awe at her daughter's minuscule size and the obstacles this preemie had to overcome—like breathing, and growing to real newborn size.

"Oh, I'm sorry, sweetie," she said, moving her face closer. "It's Momma, Tara." Jaynie traced her finger lighter than air across the child's arm, memorizing the feel. She held her breath as though Tara would break if she exhaled too hard.

Her eyes eagerly examined the bundle of life. *Mine. This is my baby.* She couldn't stop the wide smile of joy and pride that swept across her face. "Oh…" she cooed. Growing bolder, she placed her hand flat on Tara's side, savoring the warmth of her skin and the heat of the lights. "You're going to grow up to be big and strong, 'cause you're my special little girl."

Jaynie's glance danced up for the briefest of moments, to find Terrance staring at her with inquisitive deep hazel eyes. There was something troubled in his gaze. Yet he covered it up, and broke into a large grin. He clearly approved of her doting.

His hair was pulled back and tied tightly in a ponytail with a leather string at the nape of his neck, as he always wore it for work. His intense eyes took center stage, giving him a doe-eyed, beaming look—like a foolish new father.

Nah—not macho Terrance.

Besides, Tara wouldn't have a father. They'd be a family of two, and they'd make do. Just like Jaynie and her mother had. She knew from experience it wouldn't be easy, but such was life, and she'd overcome worse in her thirty-four years.

With her emotions out of control and eyes watering, she studied her child from head to toe. The tiny hand that grasped her thumb seemed to be perfection itself. Perfection, that was, until she counted the fingers. Six? What was with the extra tiny stub on the side of Tara's palm?

As though he'd read her thoughts, Terrance spoke up. "It's a common anomaly, Jaynie. They'll remove them before she leaves the hospital."

"How will they do that?" Why hadn't she planned for this?

"When they're underdeveloped, like these extra digits, I believe they tie them off with string and they literally fall off—like a skin tag."

His large fingers touched Jaynie's when he slid them over Tara's hand. They were warm. She remembered how they'd felt when he'd held her in his arms. She willfully stopped the reaction brewing in her chest.

"Will it hurt? Does it mean anything else is wrong?"

"Not necessarily," the NICU nurse broke in. "It's just a fluke of nature. It doesn't mean a thing, unless there is a history of a specific disease or syndrome. Anything unusual run in your or the father's bloodline?"

Jaynie's mind flashed to the extensive paperwork she'd received on the sperm donor's medical history. Nothing had been mentioned about birth defects or anomalies. Fear shot through her as she pondered the risk of other physical problems that might have been withheld on the sperm bank forms. But it was supposed to be the most reputable cryobank on this side of the Mississippi—that was why she'd moved to Southern California.

"I don't think so," she said.

Terrance stepped closer and smiled downward. He lifted his thick eyebrows and placed his hand before her for inspection. "See anything unusual here?"

She shook her head, feeling puzzled. All she saw was a huge hand, with long, graceful fingers, sprinkled with fine freckles and a few scrapes and scratches.

He rubbed a faint white scar on the outside of his palm. "I was born with an extra digit, too. No big deal. I turned out okay."

Boy, did he ever.

Though it was hard to tear her eyes away from her beautiful daughter, Jaynie lifted her gaze to the respiratory therapist. No, there was definitely nothing wrong with him.

He nodded his reassurance. She stepped away from the incubator and removed her mask. The sudden realization that she stood before him in a threadbare hospital gown and thin housecoat, with virtually nothing underneath other than the adult-size bladder-control-type panties, made her tense. Weak from her birthing ordeal, she couldn't muster enough extra blood to blush, so she just smiled sincerely at him. Without a stitch of make-up on, hair running wild, she was grateful for the tinted, thin black wire-framed glasses she hid behind, and hoped he hadn't noticed her ragged appearance.

The odd thing was, Terrance didn't give the impression of minding how she looked a bit. In fact, he seemed to be taking her in and enjoying every inch of her, like he always had—even after they'd stopped dating.

She squirmed a bit under his intense gaze.

The nurse brought a new bottle of total parental nutrition to replace the nearly empty IV feeding her baby. "Once she's off the ventilator, and before we've figured out if she can suck and swallow on her own, we'll start nasogastric feedings and use your milk. If her stomach tolerates it, we'll have her nursing from you as soon as possible."

The comment reassured Jaynie, and sent her over the moon with joy at the possibility of finally getting to hold and mother her baby. *Hang tough for the reward.* She repeated a chant her mother had used throughout her life.

Terrance lingered nearby, fussing with the respiratory equipment. He glanced frequently at Jaynie—she could feel it—and then he spoke.

"That's a beautiful baby you've got there," he said, with a broad, handsome smile. "You did good work."

"Thank you, Terrance. I think I'm already in love."

"With a beauty like her, I can see why." He gathered his equipment and prepared to leave, first ducking his head and searching her eyes. "She'll be fine, Jaynie." Splendid hazel-green eyes looked at her with a sincerity she hadn't expected from a macho hunk like Terrance.

"Don't worry about anything. Just concentrate on loving her. She'll feel it."

Post-partum emotion brought another rush of near-tears to her eyes. She blinked them back and swallowed. "You have no idea how much that means to me."

"Hey," he said, "what are friends for?" He patted her shoulder.

Jaynie studied Terrance in a new light: a skilled medical professional, a bit of a dare-devil and a total hunk—with a hint of compassion and a touch of empathy. Not many men had that combination of characteristics.

This slow-to-smile guy had just referred to himself as her friend. She'd always thought their effortless and casual chatter on the hospital ward had only come from a sense of civility on his part, since they'd quit dating. Yet he'd clearly defined himself as her "friend" just now. And, God only knew, she needed one today.

Jaynie had always let her witty, cynical side show for him, and he'd seemed to respond to that sense of deadpan humor that so many other people never understood. And, above everything else, a healthy and mutual respect existed for each other's medical expertise.

Both being a part of the hospital Code Blue team, they'd learned to count on each other under stress. Jaynie always felt relieved the minute Terrance showed up at any code, just as she had in the delivery room. He was also the first person she paged when things started to go downhill with any of her pulmonary patients.

"Okay." The curt NICU nurse interrupted her thought. "The love-fest is over. Jaynie, go back to your room and get some rest. Isn't it time for another fundus check?" she said, with a sparkle in her gray eyes. "I promise I'll take good care of junior, here."

As though on cue, Kim rolled the wheelchair behind her. Jaynie flopped down into it, overwhelmed with a mixture of emotions. Her very own baby, the most precious gift she could ever hope for, lay tethered to tubes and lines in a sterile hospital environment instead of nestling in the comfort of her mother's loving arms where she belonged. She patted her child one last time, memorizing the feel of her thin newborn skin covered in fine white downy hair, called lanugo.

She kissed her little one's hand and said, "Goodbye, sweetie. I'll be back later."

Tara squirmed.

Jaynie bit back her maternal need and steeled herself for better times. The life she'd planned for herself and her daughter waited just around the corner, but for now it had been put on hold.

This time she couldn't stop the tears that brimmed and spilled down her cheeks while she was rolled away from the new center of her universe. Emotionally strung out, she covered her face with her palms and let loose. One strong hand gripped her shoulder and passed her a wad of tissues. She looked up to say thanks and found Terrance, watching her with kind, empathetic eyes.

He knelt down beside her and gently wiped at her tears with a tissue he'd kept, and he looked a tiny bit misty-eyed himself.

"Hang tough, Jaynie. Tara will be home before you know it. Now, go get some rest. I'll watch Peanut."

She couldn't help but smile at his kind words. Hey, she thought with renewed optimism as she blew her nose. Her daughter already had a nickname.

"Thanks…Terrance."

CHAPTER THREE

WITH her temperature almost back to normal, Jaynie's IV was removed the next morning. She worried about her progress. Knowing how hospital census often dictated early patient discharge, she figured she'd be released after the required forty-eight-hour stay. Dread couldn't begin to describe the thought of going home without her baby. How could she face the empty nursery?

She reached for the phone. The Pulmonary Ward clerk answered in a clipped voice.

"May I speak to Kim Lee?"

It only took a moment for Annette to recognize her. "Jaynie! I'm so glad you and the baby are okay. Let me get her." Annette pushed the hold button before Jaynie had a chance to say thanks.

Close to a minute later, Kim picked up the line. "What's up, girlfriend?" Her cheerful voice broke into the up-tempo Muzak.

"Hey. Listen, you volunteered your granny to come to my house and read the Feng Shui, remember?"

"Oh, yeah-yeah-yeah."

"I want the nursery to be perfect for Tara, so could you ask her to come over tomorrow? I think I'm going to get booted out of here soon."

"I'm on it."

"You're the best." Jaynie grinned at the ceiling.

"Are you kidding? This is going to make Por Por Chang's day."

Jaynie smiled at the traditional Chinese term for the maternal grandmother. But, knowing how busy the pulmonary floor generally was first thing in the morning, she made a quick excuse to hang up.

Next, she headed for the shower.

With impeccable timing, Jaynie entered the NICU just as Dr. Shrinivasan made his morning rounds. Dressed in blue scrubs and a white doctor's coat, he sat hunched beside Tara's incubator, studiously scribbling on bright pink paper on a chart. The diminutive man finished writing a sentence on a green doctor's order sheet, and then broke from deep concentration to nod his head in greeting.

Jaynie scrubbed her hands and put on a mask, then, for good measure, put a blue paper surgical-type gown on over her street clothes, even though it wasn't necessary. With a flutter in her chest, she approached her baby.

Without introduction, Dr. Shrinivasan began to lecture in a precise, occasionally difficult to understand accent.

"Your baby is doing well. Her gestational age seems somewhere between twenty-seven to twenty-nine weeks, which gives her more than an eighty percent survival rate." He looked at Jaynie with a smile that extended to his large brown eyes. "You're a nurse, correct?"

She nodded, and tried to look at the doctor, but her gaze kept drifting to her daughter, inside the temperature-controlled, double-walled, see-through box. She stepped forward to get a closer look. Her baby had been moved into an incubator from the radiant warmer, and she knew that was a good sign—a step up. Seeing Tara flat on her back, tethered to tubes and wires, yet looking peacefully asleep, Jaynie relaxed.

"First we deal with the respiratory distress syndrome," Dr. Shrinivasan said. "Even with only mild difficulties now, she may require oxygen therapy at home. We'll see." He glanced back to Tara. "The baby is already tolerating the synchronized intermittent mandatory ventilation, which means she is taking many breaths on her own."

"May I?" Jaynie asked, before putting her hand through the porthole window to touch her daughter. He nodded. "It's Momma, Tara." She swore she saw a faint movement on her beautiful little daughter's face. "It's me. Mommy." The baby squirmed. Jaynie smiled and stroked her little arm, and noticed they'd already tied suture string around the extra finger nubs.

The doctor continued. "Her overall chances are very high. So, first we deal with the breathing. Then we tackle the immature gastrointestinal tract. She'll need to gain weight, and as you know she may lose up to ten percent of her birth weight. It takes two to three weeks to regain that." He patted her shoulder. "Slow, but sure. We'll make progress."

"How long before I can bring her home?"

"Four to six weeks. Not before she weighs four pounds. Time will tell us."

It sounded like an eternity.

Jaynie tore her eyes away from Tara just long enough to thank the doctor. He nodded and replaced the metal-backed hospital chart into its holder, then moved to the next incubator.

She stroked her baby's leg and smiled at her runty perfection. "You're doing great, sweetie." Could she survive four to six weeks without having her baby home? "Hang in," she said, mostly to herself. "Remember, I love you, Peanut."

* * *

Terrance entered the plush front office of the cryobank suite. He strolled into the flawlessly decorated room, with its comfy sofas and coffee tables covered in up-to-date magazines. Thick carpet silenced his footsteps as he approached the receptionist's window. No one was there, so he let himself in the door.

He heard a voice around the corner and followed the sound to find his friend, Dave Martinez, the sperm bank supervisor, sitting behind a large glass and chrome desk, talking on the phone. Terrance advanced and swatted a high-five greeting with his racquetball partner. Dave twisted his hand, so they could move to an old-fashioned handshake, all the while balancing the phone between his ear and shoulder, never breaking from the conversation.

Terrance waited for him to hang up. "How are you doing, man?"

"Same old, same old, T-man," Dave said.

Terrance slumped into the high-tech leather chair across from the desk. "Are we on for tonight?"

"You know I'd never miss a chance to kick your ass on the court."

"Like that would ever happen."

Terrance had danced around the real reason he'd come to talk to Dave long enough. And knowing what a stickler Dave was about the patient privacy and confidentiality state law, he figured asking out of the clear blue might give him the advantage. "Listen, I was wondering if my sperm has been used yet."

"That's highly classified information, my man. Remember, this is an *anonymous* semen donor program. You know the rules."

"I'm not asking *who* it went to. I just want to know *if* my boys got to take a swim yet, that's all." Terrance lifted one brow and gave a cocky smile.

Dave laughed, running a hand over his shiny, clean-shaven head. "Hey, your party was over the minute you left that room." He pointed to the door that closed off what was fondly referred to as the "Whoopee Room." Men entered that room armed with sterile plastic cups, provocative magazines and their imaginations, and left only after a successful "deposit" had been made. After signing on to the program, which paid participants, Terrance had been expected to make weekly contributions with a six-month commitment. He had completed his "tour of duty" a year ago.

Though impressed with the extensive medical screening he'd had to go through to donate to the sperm bank, he'd been surprised to discover he needed to write essays for the recipient, too. Penning a paragraph or two on various topics had made him feel a bit like being back in school. He'd written about his most memorable childhood experiences, who in his family he identified closely with and why, what character traits he admired in any individual, and where in the world he'd like to travel. But, most importantly, he'd written about what he'd like to pass on to his own children, even knowing he never intended to father any more.

The effort had been worth it. Just the thought of enabling a childless couple to realize their dream of having a family, anonymous or not, was reward enough.

After the loss of his own baby girl, and long after he and his wife had divorced, he'd given it a lot of thought and signed up for a vasectomy. He'd got put on a waiting list because of his age and single status. When they'd called with a surgery date, a deep primal scream from his genetic pool had protested—and he'd found himself signing on and making deposits to the sperm bank for posterity's sake before he made sure he'd never be a father himself.

Dave had offered to pay him for it, knowing he could use the extra money for his night school classes, but he'd declined. Sure, it had been a quirky, altruistic gesture—but, hey, how was a guy supposed to respond when he was giving up on his family lineage?

Now, Dave pushed back in his chair and his no-nonsense stare sent a loud and clear message. "Strict policy. No information about when or to whom your sperm gets delivered.

But you already know that. Hell, you could be a successful sperm donor a dozen times by now. But what does it matter? Theoretically, the kids aren't yours, remember?"

Knowing full well Dave's stubborn side, Terrance backed off.

Later that night, in the enclosed racquetball court at the gym, Terrance broached another subject that had been niggling in the back of his mind. He thwapped a hard, fast ball with his racket and saw a drip of perspiration fly off his head.

Steamy and hot, the room vibrated with intense competition. Rubber-soled skids, grunts and the satisfying pop of a well-hit ball reverberated around the court when the men played.

Dave lunged, but missed the return, winding up with his belly to the boards. Terrance offered his hand and hoisted his partner back to standing. A nonverbal agreement for a water break seemed in order.

After a long gulp, Terrance blurted his question. "So, what happens if one of your donors forgets to tell you about something?"

Dave swallowed his drink and poured a bit over his head. "Our screening is thorough, and we pick up any of the major problems right down to potential for color blindness." He took another drink. "Trust me, we're extensive. We would have told you if you had any possibility of major problems."

Terrance took a swing at an imaginary ball with his racket, then wiped his forehead on the shoulder of his shaggy, sleeveless gray sweatshirt. "I mean a physical trait that may have been overlooked."

"You mean like an unsightly mole on Aunt Edna's face? Or the donor had a nose job?"

"Yeah, something along those lines," Terrance said. He bent over and touched the toes of his overpriced cross training shoes to stretch out his back.

"Are you telling me you had your nose fixed?"

Terrance shot up. "Hell, no. But when I was

born I had an extra pinky finger on each hand. Evidently my grandfather did, too."

Dave tensed his eyes. "Did you willfully not tell us that?"

Terrance served with a vengeance. "Honest to God, it slipped my mind. I hadn't thought about it in years, until recently."

Dave returned the ball with a low, fast cut.

"So what now?" Terrance teased, before diving for the ball. He grunted and smashed a hit that landed way at the back line. "Are you going to throw my frozen sperm out?"

Out of breath from running fast and hard, Dave swung and hit a strong return, faking his opponent out.

Terrance growled with a swing, but missed.

"Too late," Dave said. "Donor #683 turned out to be a very popular make and model."

Dave scooped up the rubber ball and tossed it into the air for a powerful serve.

Terrance smiled to himself and swung.

Mission accomplished.

* * *

"Can't you let me stay at least another day?" Jaynie said, protesting against the inevitable the next morning with her obstetrician.

"You're in great shape. I already let you stay your guaranteed forty-eight hours. There really isn't any reason to justify your staying any longer."

"If I was in such great shape, why did I have my baby two months early, Dr. Marks?"

"We can't always explain what happens during a pregnancy, Jaynie." The tall, silver-haired woman stood before Jaynie in brown slacks, white blouse and a doctor's coat. Her brows were pinched and she looked perplexed. "Sometimes the explanation is as simple as an infection. You had a low-grade fever, and as it turns out you had a mild bladder infection. You probably just thought you were urinating a lot because of the baby." The doctor scrunched her eyes and then raised her eyebrows. "I wish I had answers for everything, but, bottom line, you delivered early, and your baby is small but healthy."

"What's your take on how long Tara will be on the ventilator?" Jaynie couldn't resist asking a second doctor, but was fearful of what her response might be.

"They want Tara to use her energy growing, not fighting for air, so they're just helping her out for a while. A week…two?"

"With all that stuff she's hooked up to, I can't even hold her." She fought the urge to cry, again, and saw the room go blurry, but refused to give in. "How does she know who her mother is?"

"She knows your voice. Just talk to her. Didn't you do that when you were pregnant?"

Jaynie nodded remembering how Tara had squirmed in the Isolette incubator when she spoke to her.

"Then keep it up; she recognizes you. There'll come a time when you'll get to pick her up and bond." Dr. Marks walked closer to the hospital bed, separated from another patient by a thin curtain, and placed her hand on Jaynie's shoulder. "Hang in. Things will work out—just not how you planned." She softened her business manner, tilted her head and looked into Jaynie's eyes with a sly smile. "Word is that they bathe the newborns in NICU at eight a.m. every single day. I'm sure they can always use an extra pair of hands—and who knows? Maybe you'll get to hold her sooner than you think."

The student nurse assigned to Jaynie's care slipped into the room with a stack of sheets in her arms.

The voice of Jaynie's roommate on the other side of the curtain pitched in. "You know, you'll be welcome to spend all the time you need in the newborn growing nursery once your baby has been moved from NICU. My first baby spent a couple of weeks there."

The young nurse piped up. "I did my last rotation in the newborn nursery. They have La-Z-Boy chairs to doze on, and the parents can come and go as they please."

The doctor listened to Jaynie's lungs and heart with a cold stethoscope bell. She made a few notations on the chart and walked towards the door. "Be sure to drink lots of water to help your milk."

"I will," Jaynie said.

The slender woman turned at the door. "I'll see you in six weeks, but call if you need anything before then."

Jaynie nodded, rolled onto her side and fought off another wave of emotion. Would her eyes ever quit tearing?

She rose, gathered her clothes and hurried toward the shower.

"Hold on, Ms Winchester," said the young nurse with huge blue eyes and shiny brown hair. "It's time to check your fundus."

"Oh, joy." Jaynie screwed up her mouth, but dutifully got back on the bed.

As the student nurse prodded and palpated her abdomen, Jaynie focused on another problem. She'd been trying to ignore the tight, heavy feeling in her breasts that she'd woken up with. But now she couldn't avoid it. Normally an average-sized woman, today she felt as if she had footballs on her chest. All she could think about was seeing Tara before she left the hospital, and using the breast pump. She'd leave her first mother's milk for when her baby would finally get fed the traditional way, through her mouth.

She needs to gain at least one pound before she'll be able to come home. Well, Jaynie thought for sure that she had at least a pound's worth of milk in her breasts right now.

After the nurse had left, Jaynie stood in the warm shower stream and tried to relax, shocked by her Pamela Anderson proportions. *My, my, my. I didn't know I had it in me.* She smiled despite the ache in her chest.

Within the next half-hour she'd dressed, got discharged from the ward, and headed down the hall to see Tara. She wore her brand new super-sized nursing bra and a button-up cotton blouse, with a pair of elastic-waist denim pants that Kim had dropped off the night before. The second most important thing she looked forward to, after bringing Tara home, was getting back to her usual one hundred and twenty-five pounds. She'd only lost ten pounds with the birth, which meant she had fifteen to go.

Once she entered the brightly wallpapered hospital nursery, all thoughts passed from her mind except for Tara. She thought of how she'd feel holding her in her arms and offering her breast to feed for the first time.

Entering the NICU, she swore Tara had already fattened up a bit. Her baby looked busy, in constant motion, stretching, twitching and jerking, swatting at the air, very much alive.

Joy jumped in Jaynie's heart at the sight. If only she could nurse her.

After cooing and patting her child, and being reassured by the nurse that all was well, Jaynie tore herself away to pay a visit to the electric breast pump. She washed her nipple with an antiseptic wipe, read the instructions on the machine, placed a small sterile plastic container on the apparatus, and plugged herself in. A strange tight suction latched on and rhythmically pulled on her tender breast. Weird sensations circulated through her flesh and head until a feeling she'd never experienced before, a soothing "let down," occurred in her milk ducts. Automatically, she relaxed.

Her mind wandered to coworkers, friends, and then back to her daughter. "If they could see me now," she mumbled with a chuckle, feeling somewhat like a dairy cow.

Being raised by a single parent herself, Jaynie had never intended to repeat her mother's plight. At least that had been her conviction until the age of thirty-three had started breathing down her neck. She'd always known she wanted to have a baby, and realized statistically it was best to be married and have both parents to share duties, but time had marched on. If she'd waited too long, she might not have ever have had a chance to be a mother.

So she'd given her boyfriend Eric an ultimatum—either they got married or broke up—but he hadn't budged, and that was the last she'd seen of him.

That was the day she'd started her research

and formed the plan to become a mom without being married. Jaynie hadn't wanted any of Eric's gene pool in her child, and she would never even have considered such a dirty trick on a man—even a conniving jerk like her ex-boyfriend. Besides, she'd needed time to increase her bank account, so she'd patiently waited.

Instead of moping around with a broken heart, Jaynie had gone to work. She'd done more research on artificial insemination and found the well-reputed sperm bank. The cost had been reasonable, its reputation flawless, the technique ethical and, most importantly, anonymous. She'd never know who the donor was and he'd never know her. And, best of all, the office was close to Mercy Hospital.

Jaynie finished pumping her other breast, then collected and labeled the tiny, plastic, four-ounce bottle to leave at the nurses' station for freezing. The container felt warm. Instead of rich thick milk, as she'd imagined, she saw thin, watery white fluid inside, like the non-fat milk she drank at home.

When she'd finished packing up, she swung the door open, stepped into the hallway—and practically bumped into Terrance's gorgeous and substantial chest.

CHAPTER FOUR

TERRANCE held Jaynie's arms to help steady her. His affable smile widened into a sexy grin. He scanned her with an easy gaze. She flushed, partly from their close proximity and the fact that he held his grip longer than necessary, and partly at being caught with breast milk in her hand.

"You okay?" He glanced at the container.

The heat spread, circling her cheeks. "Fine. I just made a deposit to Tara's trust fund." She rolled her eyes at the terrible joke, while desperately trying to draw attention away from the progressive full body-blush.

Terrance smiled before stepping back and cocking his head. "Have you been discharged from the hospital?"

"Yeah, about an hour ago." Her hands danced from her waist to behind her back, in an attempt to hide the container. She shifted her weight from one foot to the other, antsy.

"Who's taking you home?"

She cleared her throat, finding it hard to choose her words. "I'm…taking myself home. My, um, car's been in the parking lot since the other day, when I came to work."

He folded his arms. "Oh, right. Tara was a surprise." He lifted an eyebrow. "But where's her father?"

Jaynie turned her eyes away and studied her hands, once again stumped for words.

"Strike that. I've stepped over the line." He ducked his head to look into her face. "It's none of my business."

"No, it's…"

He tilted her chin up. "Being there for her delivery and all, I forgot I'm just the respiratory therapist. We quit dating and you found someone else. Forgive me, okay?"

Thoughts of missed opportunities, and

"what-ifs" flooded her brain. Tears brimmed, with annoying post-partum regularity, and Jaynie blinked a couple of times in defense. "Listen, I'd rather you hear it from me than at the hospital watercooler." She looked at her feet and the sensible walking shoes she wore. "There is no father. I'm doing this on my own."

She glanced up and saw a shift in his demeanor from concern to curiosity. She owed him an explanation, but decided not to delve too deeply.

"Tara and I are a family of two. And…I didn't get involved with anyone after you. In case that's what you're wondering."

Relief dawned on his face like a sunburst, but confusion quickly clouded his gaze.

"Well, if you were just looking for a—how shall I say it?—partner, you could have asked me, you know."

The body-blush forged into a brush fire under her skin. She made a dry swallow. "You were adamant about never wanting to be a father. Remember?"

"Right." He scratched his jaw. "Okay. Forget

I said that, let alone thought it." He looked flustered, with an appealing shade of crimson breaking across his cheeks that she suspected matched her own.

Sure, guys liked being in on the fun part, but the followthrough? Forget about it!

"The dynamic duo—Jaynie and Peanut." Terrance smiled, making it clear he wasn't making a value judgment on her decision to go it alone. "Listen, if you need any help for anything, now or later, you know my number. Feel free to call. Anytime." He stepped away, nodding toward the container in her hand. "You probably need to get that to the NICU."

Jaynie glanced at the ceiling and gave a relieved smile. "Right," she said, wishing she could get a grip on the excess emotions running rampantly in her brain.

Once she'd said goodbye, she wandered down the hall and pondered how none of the multitude of books she'd read had explained the rollercoaster ride of pregnancy, delivery and post-partum adequately.

How would she handle an empty house and nursery? Jaynie made a quick decision to close up the freshly painted and stenciled baby's room the moment she arrived home. Being there without Tara would be torture. All she wanted was the most natural desire of any new mother: to hold and nurse her baby. Yet she couldn't even do that.

Jaynie hovered over the incubator in the NICU. She wanted Tara to open her eyes and look at her, but the preemie was sound asleep. What could possibly be going on in her mind? Was she in pain? What kind of life started out being surrounded by cold, noisy monitors, blinking lights and strange hands poking and prodding, instead of feeling a mother's love and embrace?

"I'll do everything in my power to make it up to you," she murmured to her daughter.

The Feng Shui plan popped into her head, and she used the outer hallway phone to call the pulmonary floor. The ward clerk answered in her usual harried manner.

"Hey, Annette, it's Jaynie. Is Kim there?"

Maybe she couldn't hold her baby the way she wanted to today, but she would get help making her future homecoming perfect.

"What's up, Mommy?" Kim's friendly chirp answered.

"Remember the Feng Shui reading is on for tonight, right?" Dead silence. "What time are you coming over?"

"Oh, shoot. 'You Know Who' just asked me to dinner. My mind went blank and I said yes. Can we make it tomorrow night?"

Jaynie felt a rock drop in her stomach. First night home without her baby…alone.

"Never mind, I'll cancel," Kim jumped back in.

"No!" Jaynie desperately wanted company, but Kim had been practically stalking the pharmacy doc for weeks, and things were heating up between them. Opportunity seldom knocked in Kim's world of men. She'd dated some real losers.

As a friend, Jaynie didn't want to stand in her way now that the new guy was showing some potential. "Keep your date." She feigned a cheerful tone. "Tomorrow night will be fine."

After hanging up, she paced the long, narrow hospital hallway feeling adrift. She needed her baby in her arms to help her feel like a mother.

This must be how surrogates feel.

All the reading and preparing she'd done hadn't addressed the possibility of going home before her baby. She'd never even considered it. She thought about her own mother, two thousand miles away and unable to get off work until her scheduled family leave eight weeks down the line.

Feeling at odds, and unsure of what to do with herself, she made a quick decision. She'd approach one of the other mothers she'd seen in the NICU.

Her steps grew more confident as she set out on her mission to befriend another preemie mother. They might be strangers, but they had premature babies in common, to which no other person she knew could relate, and each might need the other for support.

Jaynie re-entered the quiet, institutionally drab NICU with new hope, determined to hang around for the rest of the day and form her own support group.

After comparing notes, encouraging each other, even having a long and enjoyable lunch in the cafeteria together, Jaynie and her new friend, Arpita Singh, stopped by the hospital gift store to check out the specially priced preemie car seats. She got so excited that she bought one—before figuring out how to get it all the way to the employee parking lot.

At four o'clock in the afternoon she could no longer put off the inevitable—going home. Thinking how ingenious she was, she plopped the large and awkward box into the seat of a hospital wheelchair and pushed it like a shopping cart to her car.

A dreary gray sky dripped a fine drizzle as she arrived at her SUV's trunk. She navigated the cumbersome box out of the wheelchair to the best of her ability. With legs spread wide, balancing and wrangling the cardboard container, she heard a familiar voice.

"Let me get that for you." Terrance jumped off his bike, laid it down, and quickly came to her aid. Dressed in skintight cycling shorts and a bright rainbow-colored, equally snug shirt, he wrestled the box from her arms. He lifted it like a feather, and waited for Jaynie to unlock the trunk of her car.

Like every other nurse in the hospital, she knew his routine. Run to work one day; ride his bike home. Ride to work the next day; run home. He had to be as fit as any Olympic athlete with his rigorous daily routine.

"You could have thrown your back out, trying to handle this all by yourself." He raised an eyebrow and a lightbulb went on behind his hazel lamps. "Ah, I get it. You're trying to get admitted back into the hospital, right?"

She laughed, and tried not to look at his outstanding legs. "You know, that's a thought. Gimme that back."

He pretended to fight her for it, then shoved

it into the back of her SUV, closing the hatch-back while they both laughed.

Terrance held his hand out to check on the drizzle that had quickly changed to light rain. He screwed up his face. "Could you do me a favor?"

Could she refuse the man who'd helped save her baby's life? "Sure. What do you need?"

He flashed a charming, pretty-please smile, and pointed to the sky. "A ride home?"

A sputter escaped her lips before she could compose herself. "Of course."

"So, after I spoke to Kim—" Jaynie clutched the steering wheel and took the corner cau-tiously, due to the rain "—I had to face the fact that I'd be going home to an empty house."

"Then you'll just have to have dinner with me." Terrance shifted his long legs in the passen-ger seat. "I can't let you be alone tonight." He smiled.

Jaynie nodded, never even considered pro-testing.

"Here we are." He pointed to the rustic, woodsy home almost camouflaged by over-bearing oak trees in an older neighborhood in the hills of the Silver Lake district.

She'd always thought it suited Terrance per-fectly.

"Come inside while I change?" He hopped out of the car and leaned back inside the door.

"I'll wait out here, thanks." Jaynie felt snug, and didn't want to leave the comfort of her car heater. But, more importantly, she didn't want to venture back into Terrance's territory—the world that had always been so appealing.

Now was definitely not the time to dream about a man. In fact, having just delivered her baby, it should be the last thing on her mind. And, besides, there would be no man in her carefully planned life, just Tara and her.

Terrance removed his disassembled bike from the back of her car, placed both the frame and front wheel in his garage and walked on the redbrick path toward his front porch. At the halfway point, a large, worse for wear gray cat strolled up to meet him. He bent to scratch the tabby's ears and let the pet stretch and press against his calf until the animal lost interest. Only then did he go inside.

A half-hour later, Jaynie found herself sitting across a cozy table in a hole-in-the-wall Greek restaurant on the outskirts of Hollywood, bumping knees with Terrance.

She glanced around. He had chosen the Mom and Pop eatery, and was most likely a regular, judging by the friendly greeting they'd received when they entered.

He'd changed into a cobalt-blue polo shirt, which he'd forgotten to button, affording Jaynie a glimpse of light-colored chest hair. And how could she forget the worn-to-perfection, snug-to-the-rump jeans? Looking like a classic male sculpture in modern-day clothes, Terrance had oozed confidence and seemed comfortable in his flesh when he'd walked her inside. He looked damn good in it, too, which made her ill at ease. This was not the time to notice such things—what was the point?

She finished the last of her pilaf, lamb kabob and grilled vegetables. Time had flown. They'd never lacked for conversation when dating, and ever since had maintained an easy banter at work. Tonight was no exception, and for the first time in days she felt pleasantly relaxed.

"So tell me about your cat?" she asked, before sipping her water. "I don't remember him."

Terrance wiped the corner of his mouth with a paper napkin. "His name is Papa Gino. I found him several months ago, eating from a pizza carton by one of the dumpsters at work. He was the sorriest-looking cat I'd ever seen."

Jaynie made a sad face. "Aw."

Terrance screwed up his mouth and gave her a bemused look. "So I stuck him inside my windbreaker, zipped it up and rode him home on my bike."

"Ouch. Are you serious?"

"Would I lie to you?"

She shook her head. He had a good heart, she knew that much about him, and she could trust him. He wouldn't lie. And now she had another reason to respect Terrance.

"Other than a few claw marks on my chest, he didn't seem to mind. So he's stuck around ever since, and he's good company."

She smiled.

Terrance grew serious. "Me having an independent cat is one thing." He leaned forward. "But how in the heck are you planning to raise a child by yourself?"

Jaynie brushed the tough reality check aside with a quick wave of her hand. "I've been on my own most of my life. I know the ropes; I'll make it work."

"Oh, I have no doubt that you'll rise to the challenge. It just seems like such a big responsibility." He looked into her eyes. "I admire your fearlessness."

Touched, she glanced away. "I'll be honest. I'm scared, but resourceful." She rolled her eyes and gave a courageous grin. "What I can't find out about parenting in books, I'll figure out…somehow."

He nodded his head.

His agreement gave her a false sense of confidence, but the nagging tightness in her breasts alerted her to the need to go home and pump. The last thing she wanted was to be embarrassed in public by leaking through her blouse.

"This was great, but I'd better be getting home."

"Do you have to go so soon?" Terrance sounded disappointed; it surprised her. "They've got astounding baklava here." He studied her face and must have keyed in to her unspoken need. "I'll get some take-out so you can eat it later."

"That's sweet of you, thanks." She clasped a clump of unruly hair behind her ear, wishing she'd pulled it back into a ponytail.

"I aim to please," he said, with a different kind of smile and a twinkle in his hazel eyes.

What was that about? The look took Jaynie by surprise and she had to work to ignore it. "I'm dreading walking into that house alone, but I'm really tired."

"Well, in that case, you need your rest." He

rose and pulled out her chair so she could stand, then helped Jaynie on with her jacket, lifted her hair from underneath and fiddled with it while fixing her collar.

Jaynie liked the extra attention, but ignored the chill that tickled her neck.

"I'll just have to go inside with you until you're comfortable," he said, walking away.

Terrance went to the counter, insisting on paying the entire bill, and Jaynie took the opportunity to admire his broad shoulders and narrow waist. Not to mention the threadbare denim slash high on the back of his thigh. Forcing herself to look away, she noticed the money left on the table.

Sheesh, he rescues stray cats, insists on paying the bill and is a generous tipper. Same old Terrance.

After settling the check with the owner, he met her at the restaurant door. Heavy rain, steady and cool, spilled in glass sheets from the awning. Bursting through the downpour together, he rushed her to the car by putting a protective arm around her back and holding a throwaway newspaper over her head.

When she got inside her car, she lowered the window and noticed his hair had gone wavy, plastered wet against his head. And even that looked appealing. Embarrassed, she could only imagine how *her* hair must look.

He'd led the way over the hill to the restaurant in his own hybrid car, so she wouldn't have to drive him back home.

"I'll follow you—make sure you get home safely." He didn't seem to mind standing in the weather one bit. "Angelenos don't know how to drive in the rain."

She shot him a look. "I'll be fine. You don't have to do that."

"I'm not taking no for an answer."

Too tired to think of anything smart-alecky to say, she agreed. Besides, she didn't feel like dragging that bulky car seat around. And she liked the idea of not having to set foot inside her house all by her lonesome.

On the drive home, after thinking about Tara

most of the way, and Terrance part of the way, Jaynie took the opportunity to think about snuggling up in bed and reading the book she'd borrowed from the hospital library, *Your Special Preemie.* By morning, she vowed to know everything there was to know about caring for a wee one like Tara.

Using tried and true nursing psychology, deciding to reframe the negative feelings she'd been carrying around inside, she opted to look at this particular ordeal as a great new adventure. Tara was growing in an outside womb for the last part of her gestation, and Jaynie had the privilege to watch.

Amazed by her sudden shift in attitude, and by how much better she felt, she smiled and relaxed as she rolled into her driveway.

After Jaynie had parked the car in the garage, Terrance pulled his car behind hers. The rain had let up to a fine drizzle. She popped open the back of the SUV for him, and he grabbed the box and followed her to the porch.

"Where do you want this?" Terrance angled through the front door after wiping his feet. He saw a sedately colored knitted afghan draped across an off-white overstuffed couch in the center of the room. That was new. Several matching throw rugs scattered across the hardwood floor. An old rocking chair, with flowers stitched onto the padded seat, sat beside a standing lamp complete with colorful stained glass shade, adding the only real color to the room. None of that had changed. The entire wall of bookcases, filled to capacity, seemed to be bulging with more volumes than before. And a tiny phone table with a huge vase stuffed with dried flowers was definitely new. But the feminine house seemed mostly unchanged, and he remembered how much he'd liked this older California craftsman bungalow in Glendale.

Jaynie pointed him through the large arch toward the hallway and Tara's room. "If you don't mind, I can't bring myself to go in there without her, so just set the car seat anywhere and close the door on your way out, okay?"

Little did she know how much he could relate to her concerns.

"Sure," he said, and headed down the hall.

Terrance flipped on the switch and saw a bright and happy room that sparkled and smelled of fresh paint. He grinned, even as melancholy ached in his heart.

Stenciled-on ducklings marched around yellow walls at the chair-rail line. A white enameled baby crib with an attached colorful mobile was the focus of the room. A changing table was tucked into the adjacent corner, and a tall matching dresser was placed in the other.

What a lucky kid to have a mother like Jaynie.

He eased the box to the floor, then stood with hands on hips to survey the nursery more closely. It already smelled like baby lotion and fresh fabric softener, and a vision of his daughter Emily's toothless grin appeared. He pined, and took a sniff of the baby blanket hanging across the bed rail, resisting rubbing it against his cheek—better not to wallow—and then noticing a beautifully framed picture on the wall.

Impeccable sea-blue calligraphy spelled out some words on rice paper, surrounded by a dark blue frame. It looked specially made, and he couldn't resist reading it.

And if, in the end, I've done anything worthwhile with my life, nothing will compare to this. For the greatest achievement I will claim is giving you the opportunity to exist.

His stomach dropped toward the floor when he recognized the words, no longer needing to read from the paper.

Astounding!

"'Never take life for granted,'" he repeated to himself. "'It will always outsmart you. Consider each day a challenge. Dream big, love with all your heart and think positive. Only you can write the story of your life. Make it a great one.'"

A jolt of realization struck his chest and knocked the wind from his lungs. His throat went dry and he practically lost his balance. He backed out the door, almost stumbled, trying to hide the turmoil that roared inside his head and heart.

"Are you okay?" Jaynie asked, when he returned to the living room.

"Yeah," he answered, sounding distant, as though he'd left his voice in the nursery. He brushed fingers through his wet hair. "Listen, I've got to go," he said, heading for the door. "I've got studying to do."

Terrance vaguely registered Jaynie looking confused, and thanking him for dinner on his way out. She reached for him, and he touched her fingertips with his own while backing away and wondering if she felt the shock radiating from his core.

The next few moments were a blur, until he found himself sitting in his car with the engine running.

He knew the words in the picture over Tara's bed.

Waxing poetic one afternoon in the cryobank clinic, he'd written them for his donor package.

He shook his head in disbelief.

This is astounding. I'm Tara's father.

CHAPTER FIVE

JAYNIE took Dr. Marks's suggestion and showed up at the NICU nursery at a quarter to eight—just in time for Tara's morning bath—and was rewarded with being allowed to assist while the nurse wiped and swabbed clean the baby's thin, almost transparent skin.

How feather-light she felt, and, oh, did she squirm and protest when they moved her from side to side. Jaynie grinned and giggled until tears ran down her cheeks.

This is just the way the book said bathing would go. I can't believe I'm finally almost holding her.

An amazing flood of motherhood and love overtook her, along with a hormone rush, and her eyes welled up. She bent over and pecked

Tara's cheek with the softest, sweetest kiss she'd ever given.

"I love you, Peanut."

Tara opened her puffy little eyes and stared straight at Jaynie, and she thought her heart would explode with joy.

"Hi, honey. It's Momma."

Even knowing that babies this young could only distinguish between light and dark, Jaynie still swore Tara recognized her. Her gaze seemed serious and her expression intelligent. So precious was the moment, Jaynie thought she might walk on air the rest of the day. Optimism bloomed in her heart.

All too soon the bath came to an end, and Tara got settled back down inside the incubator.

Progress. This is good.

Terrance had lain awake all night, staring at the ceiling, wondering what in the world to do about the situation. Everything had changed in the blink of an eye. He was a father again—

something he'd never intended to be after losing his little Emily.

He understood the point of donating to a sperm bank was to create babies…but not for himself. Preferring to think of it as his anonymous legacy, merely sprinkling seeds in the countryside, he had never expected to know and care about the recipient or his offspring.

Jaynie and Peanut?

He'd been told that people traveled from all over the country to use that cryobank. That was supposed to be the safeguard, and knowing whom the beneficiary was definitely wasn't part of the bargain.

He pictured tough little Tara in his mind—his daughter—and fought a smile. He *knew* he'd felt a special connection with her in the hospital nursery.

And now, though he'd resisted all night, he thought about Jaynie. She had a way of hijacking his thoughts and making his mind go blank with her natural sexy ways.

Daydreaming about a newly delivered mother? Come on. That's almost sick.

Yet he couldn't deny the lure she had for him.

The same thing had happened last night, over dinner. She had been talking away, relaxed and comfortable with their surroundings, like they were old friends. Well, hell, they *were* old friends.

If quizzed about their conversation, he'd fail. All he could remember was staring into her soft brown eyes and watching her creamy complexioned face, and the annoying warm squeeze he'd felt in his chest.

Friend wasn't the word that had come to his mind when his hand had crept dangerously close to hers on the table. Why did he always feel the urge to plant a big kiss on her? Was it the delicate groove of her upper lip that some people called a Cupid's bow? Or the sensual curl of her lower lip that drove him crazy? He remembered how they'd felt, pressed against his mouth. He shook his head and scrubbed his face, determined not to go there in his thoughts.

But it wasn't just that. He knew better. It was the whole package. Jaynie was just…well, Jaynie.

He'd been infatuated with her for over a year, not giving a second thought to the fact she was four years older than him, and when he'd finally decided to do something about the crush they'd had several terrific dates. Only problem was, she'd put herself on a fast track to motherhood. He'd had to respect her wishes, and, with him knowing he could never handle being a dad again, they'd kissed one last time and had gone their separate ways.

A few months after they'd broken up, he'd heard the hospital gossip. Jaynie was pregnant. He'd known he wasn't the father, but had privately envied whoever was.

And now he discovered he *was* the father of her child.

Astounding.

Could his mind be blown any more thoroughly?

He pressed his fingers tight against his eyelids and thought about his loss. The unending pain he felt every time he remembered Emily ripped at his heart. Clear and simple: he couldn't handle being a father. Yet everything he'd never planned or wanted in the way of parenting had already happened. He was a father. And the crazy thing was…he'd never even slept with Jaynie.

The question remained: Was he man enough to accept it?

Grateful to escape on a three-day weekend, he had big plans to rock-climb and hang-glide with Dave—far, far from Mercy Hospital. It was the personal reward he'd promised himself for doing so well on his biochemistry midterm, and he deserved it.

Jaynie—and his new responsibility as a dad for Tara—would get put on the back burner until he felt ready to deal with it.

Would he ever feel ready?

The mere thought of being a father again forced him from his early-morning torpor and out of bed to pack.

* * *

Por Por Chang entered Jaynie's house like an ancient Chinese empress. Accompanied by Kim, she bowed her head magnanimously to Jaynie. She smelled like mentholated vapor rub and sandalwood. Gray hair, pulled severely back into a tight bun, rested on a shiny Mandarin-collared, red dragon-patterned jacket.

"Welcome," Jaynie said.

Wasting no time, the bird-frail old woman walked through the house, eyes darting, hands gesturing, tongue clucking and spewing hard foreign sounds to her granddaughter.

Jaynie worked up courage and showed her into Tara's room. Again, the old woman's eyes snapped from corner to corner. More words flew out of her mouth, and Kim kept answering with, "Yeah-yeah-yeah."

She said what sounded like a mantra, "Om Ma Ni Pad Me Hum." And she made a gesture with her hand, middle fingers pointed downward, pinky and index straight out. Her thumb flicked the middle fingers and she continued to repeat the words while she paced the length and breadth of the nursery.

Fifteen minutes and a full home inspection later, Por Por Chang smiled, nodded graciously, and bowed when Jaynie offered her a cup of green tea. She sat primly on the sofa and sipped while Kim filled Jaynie in.

"First off, she did a cleansing mantra to rid the nursery of any negative energy." Kim brushed her long straight hair behind her thin shoulders, looking serious and sincere. "The crib shouldn't face the doorway. Por Por says to move it to the other wall. Negative Chi energy otherwise." Kim gave a petite swallow. "She says the color of the room is good for creativity. Add some green for health."

Jaynie smiled, feeling uplifted and encouraged about something at least.

"Overall, the *bagua* of this house is sufficient. You have good energy—Chi—flowing. But you'll need to bring more color in for happiness and health." She glanced toward her por por, who encouraged her with a nod. "Bring in more of the five elements: fire, earth, metal, water, wood. And never keep anything dead inside. You must replace your dried flowers with a real plant to intercept the bad energy. And put a fountain somewhere. Even a small one will do."

Por Por Chang pinched her lips into a tiny smile, pleased with her granddaughter's interpretation. Only then did Jaynie realize the older woman could understand English.

As they left, Kim whispered into Jaynie's ear, "I'll fill you in on my date later." They hugged goodbye. "Do you want to have lunch Sunday at the hospital? It's my weekend on."

"Sure," Jaynie said, knowing she'd be visiting Tara, and glad to have plans of any kind to keep from rattling around in her empty house.

Once they'd left, she set to work rearranging the nursery. She hung the special essay from her sperm donor on another wall and reread its content, feeling a wealth of emotion.

What kind of wonderful man could write those words?

And, when she was done, she made plans to visit the local bookstore the next day, to buy a book on Feng Shui.

On Sunday, Jaynie found herself looking for Terrance in the NICU, but he was nowhere in sight. Tara fidgeted and squirmed when she first arrived, fussed while she bathed her and then settled down when Jaynie pressed her hand gently over her tummy and spoke soothingly to her in mommy language. Unknowingly, they had already slipped into a routine.

When Tara was fast asleep, Jaynie called Kim in Pulmonary and met her for lunch.

She continued to watch for Terrance in the hospital cafeteria, where she dined with her friend on macaroni and cheese, salad, and canned fruit cocktail in jello.

"Tommy finally asked me out for a Saturday night—a weekend date. Can you believe it?" Kim's dark almond eyes sparkled with excitement. The totally white uniform seemed to make her glow.

"Fantastic." Jaynie realized how different their situations were. Kim dreamed of finding the right man, and Jaynie needed to learn to live completely without one.

"Yeah-yeah-yeah. He's taking me to see *Mamma Mia!* Don't you think that's a step up on the dating scale?"

"Definitely."

A flash of a cozy Greek café and a handsome male face popped into Jaynie's mind. In the midst of discovering motherhood, an odd craving for something beyond Mediterranean food, something in tight jeans and a blue polo shirt, puzzled her. Now was definitely not the time for such fantasies.

Terrance squinted into the early-morning glare on this crisp, clean Sunday in Joshua Tree state park. Making like Spiderman up the side of a cliff was exactly where he wanted to be. Elevated two hundred feet, and concentrating deeply on each fissure in the wall of rock, he chose a crack and inserted the fingers of one hand. Next he planted his smooth-soled boot on a cleft below, and placed his other hand in a chink slightly above the opposite hand, moving the second foot to a credit-card-thin ledge. His friend Dave followed.

So far, so good.

He searched and reached up to a split in the granite, but his hand slipped on slick rock and his foot slid off. He swung loose, left to dangle in his harness on the sturdy rope he'd anchored above. It gave a couple of inches.

With skyhook in hand, and ready for action, he felt adrenaline rush through his veins. He swung, to latch on to something…anything. This was what he lived for—the excitement of man against the elements, the draw of danger.

"I'm okay," he called out to Dave. His eyes swept below and noticed a huge crevasse. If he fell right now, at the height and angle he was hanging, he'd be seriously injured. Maybe even killed.

Two thoughts popped into his head. Jaynie and Tara.

Astounding.

Arriving back to work early Monday morning, Terrance came to find out that three of his respiratory therapists had decided to make it a three-day weekend. The night shift supervisor had pre-arranged for registry staff to fill in, but that meant that *he* would have to work the NICU and face his demons—namely the cherubic Tara and her sexy mother.

Fighting off an illogical desire to run directly to Tara's incubator and coo at her, he went systematically through each baby in the unit. He checked the ventilators and performed the daily arterial blood gases, having to prick tiny capillaries in the preemies' heels and causing general uproar around the unit. Finally, he reached his secret daughter.

He approached with a smile, but it quickly faded when he saw that Tara wasn't sedated enough, and that her efforts to breathe weren't synchronized with the ventilator pressure. Her oxygen saturation read right at the ninety percent mark, occasionally dipping below.

"Natalie?" he called to the nearest NICU nurse. "When was baby Winchester last medicated? She's way too active."

First he checked for air leaks, making sure the tube in her trachea fit properly, and that there was no need to place a larger one. No problem there.

The ventilator made peeps and pings as he adjusted the pressure down and the oxygen concentration up a minute amount. He knew how important the right combination was to maintain proper lung function without causing injury to the delicate tissues.

Over-oxygenation in a preemie could also cause damage or scarring to the tiny capillaries in the eyes. He kept that in mind, and only made the smallest adjustments.

He used his stethoscope to listen to Tara's lungs and heard a disturbing sound in her right lower lobe. Nothing. He listened again. No movement of air in or out suggested a collapse in a portion of her lung. Air collected and trapped in her chest could interfere with her heart and lung function, and he knew the condition needed immediate attention.

"Did they do today's chest X-rays yet?"

The nurse nodded, while drawing up some medication to insert into Tara's intravenous line.

Terrance paged Dr. Shrinivasan, rechecked Tara's pulse-ox readings, and then went searching for the latest chest film.

Instead of answering the page, Dr. Shrinivasan appeared, almost miraculously, on the ward.

"Doctor S." With a grim look, Terrance handed the X-ray to the specialist. "It looks like a pneumothorax has developed."

"How large?" The doctor raised his brows and slapped the film into the bright viewbox on the wall. He clicked his tongue while he studied the X-ray. "We'll need to insert a chest tube."

Terrance alerted Natalie, who brought a prepackaged chest tube tray and suction machine, while the doctor scrubbed his hands and placed sterile gloves on. Terrance did the same.

"Call the mother—let her know what we're doing," Dr. Shrinivasan said to the nurse.

Consulting the X-ray, he drew an "x" where it would be best to insert the tube, into the space between two ribs on Tara's side. She'd already settled down from the sedation, but squirmed when Terrance put a cold betadine swab next to her skin.

He wiped in a circular motion, starting at the center and moving concentrically outward. Then he repeated the process two more times, to make the procedure as close to sterile as possible. He put a blue paper sterile field with a hole in the middle over her body.

Dr. Shrinivasan worked like the skilled professional he was, and in no time the chest tube had been expertly inserted. Terrance taped it in place. The results were immediate and amazing. With the tube and suction relieving the excess air pocket, the compressed lung would be able to re-expand. The leaking air sacs would now have a chance to heal over the next couple of days.

Tara's oxygen saturation moved back up over the ninety percent mark and the ventilator quit squawking.

While Terrance readjusted the settings on the ventilator, Dr. Shrinivasan approached.

"You were very helpful today. As always. I'm glad you have decided to attend medical school."

"Oh, hey—thanks, Doc S. Your vote of confidence means a lot to me."

"If you'd like, I will make a recommendation at the University Medical School affiliated with Mercy Hospital. Instead of having to leave the state, you could continue living and working here."

The compliment was greater than Terrance could ever have imagined. He shook the doctor's hand and thanked him profusely.

"Now," Dr. Shrinivasan said, "do you want to call this baby's mother and tell her the successful news? Or shall I?"

Under normal circumstances only Dr. Shrinivasan would have done any updating on infant conditions. Terrance realized even the doctor had figured out that something more than the ordinary was going on between Terrance, Jaynie and Tara.

"You better do it, doc," he said, gathering his equipment and moving on to the next incubator, with plans to be out of the unit before Jaynie arrived.

He wasn't yet ready to face the woman who unknowingly had changed the course of his life.

As Dr. Shrinivasan had promised Jaynie, the chest tube got removed three days later, and Tara seemed surely set on the road to progress. But Terrance was nowhere in sight. The good doctor had explained everything to her so thoroughly, she couldn't even manage to come up with a fake question as an excuse to call Terrance.

Another few days passed in comforting routine. Jaynie never so much as glimpsed Terrance, and chose to concentrate on her new life and daughter.

The following Monday morning, her phone

rang, waking her up. She looked at the clock, surprised by how late she'd slept: seven-thirty a.m.

When she answered, Terrance's deep, soothing voice vibrated on the other end. "I thought you'd want to be the first to know that I just extubated Tara."

Jaynie gasped.

"She's off the respirator and breathing on her own," he said. "Beautifully."

"I'll be right over," Jaynie said, throwing back the covers and sitting up with lightning speed.

An hour later, when she entered the NICU, Terrance had stuck around. With dark circles all the way to his cheeks, he looked exhausted. Avoiding her stare, he smiled, but it didn't reach his eyes. He seemed tentative and distant. Too excited about Tara to stop, Jaynie disregarded his troubling appearance and flew past, brushing his hand on the way to her daughter's incubator.

Sure enough, in no sign of distress, her

baby slept with a knit cap perched on her head and the tiniest pacifier Jaynie had ever seen plugged into her mouth. Her tiny lip twitched and drew intermittently on the rubber binky, sucking like a newborn on a learning curve. The respirator had been replaced with a minute oxygen cannula, resting beneath her nose, and a tiny feeding tube inserted into one of Tara's nostrils. How they could find a catheter small enough to fit amazed Jaynie.

"Oh, my Lord, I can't believe it." Joy leapt in her heart. She clutched the incubator to keep from floating away. More tears—the good kind—washed down her cheeks.

Dr. Shrinivasan approached. "We're feeding her your breast milk through the nasogastric tube. It will help with digestion and the lining of her intestines." He patted her arm in a fatherly fashion and nodded. "We want to encourage the sucking reflex. This is so far and so good."

He squinted his eyes and gave a pleased smile, bobbing his head from side to side. "This will also help improve her blood oxygen level. We will observe her progress." With hands crossed behind his back, he turned to leave, but first raised a finger. "One very reputable study showed that breast-milk-fed preemies go to their homes fifteen days sooner than formula babies."

Jaynie wanted to hug him, but refrained. Her hands slipped into the portholes on the incubator and she stroked Tara's tummy and whispered soothing words, then kept vigil for the next several minutes until the breast milk disappeared.

She wanted to thank Terrance for calling her, and share the good news about Tara's progress with him. But when she turned he was nowhere in sight, and she figured he probably already knew, anyway.

Filled with delight and new hope, she hugged her newest friend, Arpita, when she arrived later for her daily visit. Unfortunately, little Manish, her son, wasn't progressing as quickly as Tara. Jaynie felt some of her joy dissipate when she saw the preemie's little ribs retracting and struggling with each breath, and the worried look in Arpita's huge brown eyes.

Later, tears filled those doe eyes as Arpita told Jaynie that Manish had developed a respiratory infection during the night. Jaynie put her arm around her new friend and offered a shoulder for her to cry on, and before long joined her.

Exhausted, and on her way home for lunch and a nap, she glimpsed Terrance at the other end of the hall. He looked preoccupied with another employee, and she didn't want to interrupt, so she left without saying goodbye.

Kim had the day off. She'd give her a call after talking to her mother long-distance, and she would tell Kim all about Tara's progress. And then she'd talk her into shopping for some pillows, paint and a small indoor fountain for her house.

"Each day is one step closer to bringing Tara home," she chanted like a mantra. "One step closer to bringing Tara home."

* * *

The next morning, both a new R.N. and R.T. were assigned to the NICU. Jaynie wondered where Terrance was, and why he hadn't been coming around. But she soon got distracted when the older nurse approached her with a sparkle in her eye and a tiny bath blanket tucked under her arm.

The nurse wisely stood back and let Jaynie do the entire a.m. care for Tara, who reacted to her mother's attention with squirms, and made a tiny bleating sound.

Jaynie laughed.

"Oh, my gosh, she sounds like a little lamb." She smiled and touched her index finger to Tara's delicate chin, and the baby opened her mouth as if she wanted to eat. Jaynie slipped her pinky finger inside. Tara latched on. Surprised, Jaynie's eyes widened, and she turned to the R.N. who nodded in approval.

As the morning progressed, Tara got fussy and couldn't seem to settle down.

"I want you to go pump yourself." The nurse

spoke in gentle tones. "We'll try an experiment."

When Jaynie returned, a rocking chair had materialized and the nurse handed her an adult-sized bath blanket. "Now, open your blouse, take off your bra and sit down," she said.

The R.N. went about untangling Tara from all of the tubes and wires strategically placed around her body, holding her like a football, and then put her against Jaynie's chest, smack between her breasts. She wrapped the blanket around Jaynie's middle, swaddling child to mother.

"This is called Kangaroo-care. Two doctors from South America discovered in the 1980s the amazing results of keeping preemies close to their mothers' skin." She winked and nodded at Jaynie. "See—it's like a pouch."

The feel of her own flesh and blood flush to her chest brought an incredible sense of peace. Her breasts tingled as if her milk was about to let down, and she was grateful that she'd just used the pump. The nurse placed a second bath towel over Jaynie's shoulders like a shawl, and she settled in to rocking and humming to her daughter.

Within seconds Tara relaxed, and drifted off to sleep, allowing Jaynie to study her close up, press her to her bosom for warmth and kiss the top of her perfect little head.

"This will help your baby conserve her energy for growing, both physically and emotionally," the nurse said with a kind, knowing smile, "while maintaining good body temperature."

The peace of finally holding Tara the way she had dreamed, feeling her fine skin and warmth, acted like a drug. Before long, with her arms wrapped securely around her tightly swaddled child, Jaynie drifted off to sleep, too.

Terrance couldn't stay away any longer. It had been days since he'd gone to see Tara and he couldn't stand the separation. The same blood in her veins ran in his, and her precious preemie soul called out to him. Since returning from his rock-climbing trip he'd made a point to only come around when Jaynie wasn't there—which was hard, because she always seemed to be there.

Today wasn't even his day to cover the baby ward. He'd only been passing by, but he wanted to check on his daughter. Plus, he had a zebra-patterned soft toy to deliver. One of the NICU nurses had explained that newborns responded to that pattern and it was good for infant eye development. And so he couldn't resist a visit.

With impeccable timing, Terrance rounded the corner and observed the most riveting sight of his life. There before him sat Jaynie Winchester, bare-shouldered and wrapped in a sarong made out of a thin hospital bath blanket. Tara's tiny head was wedged between her full breasts. The most incredible look of contentment graced Jaynie's face as she looked down at the baby tucked snugly to her chest. At first he thought she was nursing, and he panicked, tried to retreat, but couldn't bring his feet to move.

Seeing Jaynie and Tara before him, a modern-day portrait of Madonna and Child, he stood dead in his tracks. He couldn't manage to turn himself in the other direction and race out of the room, like any gentleman would.

Jaynie's head of soft, full curls outlined her face and fell across her shoulders. Her eyes were serenely closed. Running the risk of being a shameless voyeur if he didn't do something besides stand there and ogle a half-dressed woman—who happened to be the mother of his child—Terrance cleared his throat and prepared to speak. But then thought better of it.

Overwhelmed with emotion, coupled with days of insomnia and soul-searching over life and his priorities, and people he cared about, he felt his eyes go blurry. He sniffed and swallowed, and fought the surge of feelings.

Astounding.

Wanting simultaneously to curse Jaynie for messing up his plans, and rush to her side to tell her he was Tara's father, Terrance withstood the urge, knowing it would only complicate things further. Jaynie had never meant to become anything more than a family of two. Butting into her dreams and plans with his sperm donor news would only mix her up. And Lord only knew he was mixed up enough for both of them. She deserved more than that, and she needed all of her energy to deal with being a mother for Tara. No, it wasn't fair to drop a bomb like that and run.

And, besides, he still wasn't sure if he wanted to be a real father. As long as he kept the information to himself, he had an option to back out, without ever hurting Jaynie or appearing like a coward.

If he didn't think he could stand the responsibility of fatherhood, the risk of loving someone more than life itself and the pain of loss, he could retreat with his macho pride. And he had out-of-state medical school interviews to prepare for as a distraction.

The usual excitement he felt when he thought about his future didn't manage to rally itself while he stood there watching Jaynie and Tara.

Instead, his heart ached with a strange sense of yearning.

He took one last look at what should be the center of his universe and made a decision. He wouldn't tell Jaynie he was the father…not yet. First, he needed more time to sort out his feelings for her and their child. And he could give Tara the zebra toy another day.

Another week passed and Tara was showing great promise, with a few ounces of weight gain and a stronger rooting reflex. Every time Jaynie swaddled and held her the little mouth seemed to search for a nipple, and on several occasions, with the nurse's encouragement, she had offered herself for Tara's exploration. Jaynie dreamed of the day when she'd finally get to nurse her.

"When we go home, you'll have your own room, and lots and lots of toys." Jaynie spoke quietly to her snoozing baby. "You'll get to eat and sleep all you want—"

"Speaking of eating—" Terrance's deep voice interrupted.

Jaynie's glance shot across the room, finding him instantly. Her eyes went wide, and a tiny gasp escaped her lips. "Oh, hi."

Reaching lightning-fast for a small cotton blanket, she draped it over her shoulder, covering both her and Tara. A flush of heat rose up her cheeks.

"Hi," he said.

Tara jerked her head and Jaynie smoothed her fingers over the baby's neck to help settle her down.

"I'm really sorry," he said, raising his hands and moving closer. "I didn't mean to interrupt anything, but to be honest you stunned me." His face flushed, which struck her as odd. "I didn't mean to frighten you."

"No, you didn't." She smiled and shook her head. "I haven't seen you in forever. Have you been away on a big adventure? Waterfall-surfing or something?" she teased, with a playful glance his way.

He scratched his jaw. "Now, that sounds like it has possibilities." His eyes searched for hers, and when they met, she was struck by the change in his look from horsing around to dead serious. "Actually, I thought it was about time I took you out for another meal. You're looking skinny— except for that large growth on your chest."

She flashed a look at her ample cleavage over the top of the swaddling blanket, with Tara's head tucked between, and subtly pulled it up a bit higher. Terrance's cheeks grew the faintest shade of pink.

"I didn't mean those… I meant that…" He scrubbed his hand across his face and grimaced.

Jaynie laughed at how he'd put his foot in his mouth…again. But Terrance recovered quickly.

"I meant the little bundle there." He pointed toward Tara. Serious again, he continued. "Anyway, how about it?" He clapped his hands together. "Will you have dinner with me tonight, after I get off work?"

Tara startled. Jaynie soothed her.

Terrance covered his eyes and grimaced— again. Sorry, he mouthed.

Jaynie had been spending a lot of time in the nursery, and even more time alone at home. The thought of keeping company with Terrance had a certain appeal.

"Thanks for asking. I'd like that. I'll need to go home and change, so you can pick me up there."

Judging by the smile on his face, she'd given the right answer.

CHAPTER SIX

JAYNIE put her arm around Arpita as the doctors whisked Manish off to surgery. "What's going on?"

Arpita wrung her hands. "He started passing blood in his diapers. They said he needs surgery for a blockage." She burst out in tears. "What am I going to do?"

Jaynie's nursing background had her thinking it was necrotizing enterocolitis causing little Manish's problems. The earlier respiratory infection hadn't helped his oxygen level in the least, and she also knew he was anemic on top of that. Adding it all together, his colon had most likely developed an area of weakness, and, being opportunist, bacteria probably found a place to thrive. Manish had been looking bloated and uncomfortable recently. At a mere two and a half pounds, and eating poorly, things must have gotten worse. The surgeon would need to remove the area in question, which would mean an even longer struggle to survive, thrive and finally go home.

Poor Manish.

Jaynie held Arpita's tense fists and tried her best to offer silent support until her husband, Baldeep, and her mother-in-law arrived. After that, Jaynie sat on pins and needles beside Tara's bed, praying for surgical success for Manish, and waiting for news.

That evening, no one answered the door at Jaynie's when Terrance knocked. He tried again. Nothing.

If she's not here, she must be at the hospital.

He hopped into his hybrid car and headed for Mercy.

Just before arriving at the NICU, Terrance saw and recognized a couple leaving the ward. The husband supported the wife, who was crying and nearly hysterical. "Baldeep," she croaked between gasps. "Why?"

A pained look drew Baldeep's large black eyes together as he wrapped his arms around the young woman. "He was too small, Arpita. Too young."

Her lively colored sari seemed sadly out of place as he led her away.

Terrance clenched his jaw and his stomach knotted. He knew what they were going through all too well.

He entered the unit and found Jaynie sitting and rocking, looking stunned. Her hand rested carefully on Tara's isolette for support. A cascade of tears ran down her flushed cheeks.

He rushed to her and knelt, but didn't need to ask what was wrong.

She stared straight ahead, devastated. "Manish died in surgery." Jaynie removed her glasses, covered her face with the crumpled tissue she clutched in her hands and wept.

Lifting her to stand, Terrance guided her to the R.T. blood gas room for privacy. After closing the door, he drew her to his chest. She hugged her arms to her heart and buried her head in his shoulder. Rocking to and fro, he stroked her soft curls with one hand and smoothed her back with the other.

He inhaled the fresh scent of her hair and skin, and wanted more than anything to take away her pain. He kissed the crown of her head and squeezed her tighter, feeling her tremble beneath his grasp. The depth of her sadness took his breath away. He knew this pain—pain that ripped the air from your lungs, strangled your heart and took your will to live away. He fought a wave of nausea and concentrated on Jaynie.

She turned her head and tucked herself under his chin, easing her arms around his back.

God, he loved how she felt. An intense desire to comfort her helped him focus solely on the lady in his arms.

"I'm so sorry, Jaynie. I'm sure they did everything they could to save him."

Jaynie gulped and wiped at her tears. "He was so precious and helpless."

...and there was nothing you could do to stop it.

Terrance recalled the last night he'd put Emily to bed. His ex-wife had had a headache, and he'd volunteered for the job. Her precious gurgles and sparkling elfin eyes had looked at him with all the trust in the world. She'd been teething, and had needed some baby medicine.

He'd played with her chubby toes while he changed her diaper, and his ex-wife had scolded him from the other room. "Don't get her all riled up."

He'd looked at Emily and poked her belly button. "I'm not getting you all riled up, am I?"

She'd let out an ecstatic squeal, and he'd shushed her, just before he'd kissed her goodnight...

He kissed Jaynie's forehead and she looked into his eyes, saying, "I don't think I could survive if Tara died."

Biting back the pain that squeezed his chest, he grazed her smooth cheek with his own and whispered into her ear, "Then we'll just have to make sure that Tara will always be fine."

She turned her face ever so slightly, as if she meant to say something. The move brought their lips together. Tentative, as though it was a mistake, he waited for Jaynie to withdraw. She didn't. Then in a rush, their mouths merged, warm, soft and open, like lovers.

Like parents, united by tragedy.

Hesitant to overstep his bounds, he held back, soon realizing she didn't seem to mind. Terrance tested the velvet-smooth warmth of Jaynie's mouth. His gentle kisses turned intense and deep. He found her tongue and explored with his own, savoring the sweet taste. His body flushed with fire when he nibbled the soft pads of her lips and tasted the salt from her tears.

In a flare of excitement she kissed him back, moving her arms from around his waist to his neck. Her warm hands drew him downward and pressed his face closer to hers. Pulling her flush to his chest, he sensed the heat of her breasts, running his hands up her sides, then turning his head to delve deeper into her luscious mouth. The tip of her tongue pressed firmly against his, she brushed and swirled, and he heard himself groan in response. They'd crossed over the line from comfort kiss to raw passion.

Desire ran deep, but, remembering where they were, he regrettably tore himself away.

Breathless, and stunned by what had just happened, he found it hard to focus. Jaynie rested her head on his chest again, this time more relaxed. Perhaps the kiss was exactly what she'd needed. He forced his racing pulse to slow down and embraced her for several more moments, memorizing every tantalizing second of their encounter. He inhaled her sweet fragrance, and when she had had enough he pressed his lips to the crown of her head one last time.

She looked up and smiled at him with wide brown eyes. "Thank you for being here for me," she said.

"What are friends for?"

They both chuckled at his misstatement.

He grew serious, and tried again. "I can't think of any place else I'd rather be."

He saw the look of deep appreciation in her gaze, and longed for something more. He longed to tell her the truth about the situation. But things were too complicated, and he had too many secrets. And one of them—*I'm the donor*—could blow their friendship off the planet for good.

They held hands and went back inside the NICU. They watched Tara's perfection for several more minutes, which gave Terrance a chance to digest what had just happened.

"Look," she said, "her little extra fingers are gone."

He nodded, and thoughtlessly rubbed the faint scars on his own hands. Evidence of the gene he had given her.

When Jaynie's stomach growled, he gently bumped her with his shoulder. "Let's go eat."

She didn't argue.

Later, when he walked her to her door, he didn't press his luck with another kiss. But one thing was for sure: his feelings for Jaynie went beyond infatuation, and he intended to explore their depth. He owed that much to himself.

They had avoided the subject of the kiss over dinner, and spent most of the evening talking about Manish, and Arpita and Baldeep's grief. And, of course, they'd talked about Tara.

Just before Jaynie unlocked her door and prepared to go inside, he noticed a large box on the doorstep. "What's this?"

"Call me crazy, but I bought a satellite dish so I can watch the baby channel. Tomorrow I'm planning to call a handyman to set it up. Or maybe I'll save the money and do it myself. It comes with instructions."

"I'm off tomorrow." He'd postpone his plans to write up his latest biochem lab results and study for the upcoming test. "Just say the word, and I'm all yours."

She narrowed her eyes and half smiled. "I couldn't ask you to do that."

"Why not? Do you think I'd let you climb on

the roof and risk breaking your neck so Tara can be an orphan?"

"So I should let *you* risk breaking *your* neck?" she said, incredulously.

"I'm a guy. I was born to climb roofs, sweetheart." He gave a lopsided grin and hopped onto the porch railing, then hung from the eave, swinging and showing off like a cocky teenager. *The silly things she brought out in him.*

Gimlet-eyed, she beamed, and Terrance thought he detected a spark he'd never seen before. He hoped it had something to do with their kiss.

After dangling awhile, giving Jaynie a chance to think, he swung down, landing directly in front of her. She took a tiny step back. Her glance darted to her toes.

"What time do you want me?"

"I'll be home from Tara's bath by ten," she said, lifting her head.

"I'll be here." He winked, and darn if she didn't blush. He liked that.

Jaynie ran her hand along her neck and

looked flustered. A moth piloted past her head on its way toward the porch light. Jaynie's smile made Terrance want to grab her and start kissing her all over again, but he swatted at the moth instead.

"Okay, then," she said.

He had no intention of moving until she closed the door. "Okay." He grinned back like a kid, cupping the moth in his fist, resisting the tickle in his palm, savoring the look on her face.

Her eyes widened and she shook her head. "Okie-dokey," she stuttered. "G-goodnight." And she closed the door.

He stood his ground for several seconds, saw her turn around and lean against her hands on the thick beveled glass door, and when he listened carefully he thought he heard her sigh.

Then he released the captured moth into the night, and followed it home.

Promptly at ten a.m. on a bright and crisp spring morning, Terrance showed up wearing a sleeveless tee shirt and jeans with rips in both knees. A utility belt with an assortment of tools graced his narrow hips. Instead of being pulled back in a tight, low ponytail, his hair hung loose.

Jaynie caught her breath at the sight. She'd been reeling over their passionate kiss all night, and wondered how she could have acted so wantonly in a hospital, after her friend's baby had just died. Confusion over Terrance and what he did to her didn't even scratch the surface of the emotions battling inside her head.

Tanned, muscular arms and hands lifted the satellite dish out of the box with ease. A long leg and strong thigh used the veranda rail as leverage to boost both him and the equipment onto the roof.

He didn't even need a ladder.

Jaynie ignored the flutter of dueling hummingbirds in her chest, and fought off a sigh and a good old-fashioned breast-heave. "Holler if you need anything."

"Sure will," he said.

She closed the screen, but left the door open, and went to the kitchen to make him pancakes. The least she could do was feed him.

Forty-five minutes later he tapped on her screen door. Two lines of sweat streaked both temples. All man. She caught a whiff of his pheromones, and almost felt her milk let down.

He wolfed down the buckwheat pancakes she'd made for him, gulped the fresh-squeezed OJ and grinned. "Thanks. That was fantastic. Now, let's check out your new TV channels," he said, and slid back the kitchen chair.

Following his lead, she joined him in the other room. And over the next several minutes they watched a woman demonstrate how to make homemade baby food, using some fancy steaming tray, a hand-cranked gizmo that cost $19.99 and fresh vegetables.

Interrupting her thoughts about making baby food, the message from her chest came loud and clear. Time to pump.

Realizing she couldn't put it off any longer,

Jaynie hesitated. "I'm…um…going to have to pay a visit to my…thingie." She waved her hand toward her bedroom and felt her cheeks flame up.

Clueless, he studied her like a partner in charades, waiting for the next clue. "Your 'thingie'?"

"You know that, that…deal I used in the hospital?" she stammered. "The machine?" She caught herself placing her fingertips over her chest, and quickly stuck her hands in her jean pockets.

He glanced at the front of her blouse with sloe eyes, comprehension dawning and torturing her.

"It's…um…" She rolled her eyes and whispered, "Time to pump."

Unable to help himself, he teased her with a crooked, playful smile. "Don't mind me—go right ahead. I'll be writing down the recipe for sweet potato puree. Like she says—" he nodded toward the television and winked "—it's loaded with beta carotene."

"Terrance," she chided, and he relented, instead looking over at two cans of crimson paint, and a drop cloth in the corner of the living room.

"Planning on painting?"

"Yeah," she said, and motioned. "That wall—this weekend."

"Can you save it for Monday? It's my weekend on."

She thought fast. "I can manage by myself."

He moved closer. "I'm offering to help. Be gracious and accept. Besides, it will give you more time with Tara this weekend."

She battled her usual stubborn resolve to be completely independent with the chance to spend more time with Tara—not to mention time alone with Terrance again.

"Well, now that you put it that way," she said, feeling somewhat foolish. "Okay." What could the harm be? Painting a wall with a friend? A hunky friend at that.

Neither of them had mentioned the kiss from the night before, but Jaynie thought for sure his eyes watched her mouth a lot more than any regular friend would. Still tingling from his touch, she caught her lower lip with her teeth and noticed he did the same. Her mouth grew dry and she licked her lips, then immediately stopped herself, horrified by how it must look to Terrance. A shiver tickled through her and her milk let down.

Her eyes shot open, and before damp circles could spread out across her shirt she said, "Oh, I've got to go." She ran to her room, shirking her hostess duties, leaving Terrance to let himself out.

And, if she wasn't mistaken, she heard him chuckle when he left.

Jaynie got a shock the next day when she went to visit Tara. After scrubbing her hands like a surgeon, and entering the unit, she found Tara's isolette wasn't in its usual spot. A quick jolt of terror made her stop in her tracks. Quickly one of the regular nurses caught her arm and led her toward the back door.

"She's been moved to the growing nursery. Tara has graduated from the NICU."

Joy replaced fear and filled Jaynie's heart, pumping excitement through her veins. She rushed to the other room and was rewarded with a vision of serenity. Tara lay flat on her back, pacifier in her mouth, with far fewer wires and tubes tethering her tiny body. Her IV and heart monitor leads had been removed. The only thing remaining was the nasogastric tube and an oxygen saturation monitor taped to her foot. She lay peacefully asleep, tucked beneath a thin cotton blanket. Her knit cap remained snug on her head.

Jaynie's favorite nurse, the one who had introduced her to Kangaroo Care, greeted her by the incubator. They hugged like old friends.

"When she wakes up, I think it's about time to put Tara to breast," the nurse said.

Gasping at the wonderful news, Jaynie squeezed the older woman's arm. She smiled at her daughter, almost willing her to wake up, and within a few minutes Tara's hazel-tinted eyes appeared beneath paper-thin lids.

The nurse explained about nutritive versus nonnutritive nursing. "More than likely, she'll just play at it at first. But all sucking is good for her."

After changing Tara's diaper, the nurse gestured for Jaynie to sit in a La-Z-Boy chair, and handed the baby into her eager arms. She pressed her nipple to Tara's lips, amazed at the instantaneous response from the baby. She latched on with gusto and sucked as if she'd been doing it since birth. She giggled at the sight, and heard a quiet chuckle from the nurse.

"She's a pro," the nurse announced as she washed her hands. Then she walked to another layette and newborn, leaving Jaynie and Tara to nurse in peace.

Tara's little head soon lolled back, breaking suction from her mother's breast, making a small popping sound. Jaynie smiled benevolently. "You're not done yet, Twiggy. We've got to fatten you up so I can bring you home," she cooed.

A lost cause, Tara was out to the world. Jaynie stood and replaced her sleeping baby in the isolette. She closed the flaps on her nursing bra and started buttoning up her blouse.

One of the nurses called out. "Hey, Terrance. What's shakin'?"

"Not much, Peggy. How's Peanut?"

Jaynie smiled at the sound of his voice. Eager to say hello herself, she immediately turned. "She's doing great," she said in a loud whisper. "Come and see for yourself."

Oh, he'd seen for himself, all right. The tempting bulge of cleavage he glanced just before Jaynie refastened the last button on her blouse, and the reaction he'd felt throughout his body, had taken him by surprise. This was a side of Jaynie he'd never seen before, had only fantasized about, and the turn-on shocked his sensibilities right down to his low-cut athletic socks.

His face grew hot.

Astounding.

Terrance Zanderson, flustered by the sight of a partially exposed woman? Not likely. He'd never had any problems getting or keeping a woman naked. But this woman was different. This was Jaynie, looking more sensual than he'd ever seen her before. And for once she wasn't wearing her glasses. Her deep brown eyes had a decided look of nearsightedness, with large black pupils and the hint of a squint as she tried to see him more clearly. The term *bedroom eyes* came to mind, and that was exactly where he wanted to be…with her. Right now.

"I think we should go have lunch," he said, searching for anything to disrupt the direction of his thoughts.

"Hey, that sounds great," she said.

He'd never seen her smile so freely, and again he felt himself taken aback at her natural loveliness. Her wonderfully full mouth spread across a white, slightly imperfect overbite. Far beyond a *nice* smile, it was a *great* smile, and he longed to see it every day…for the rest of his life.

Now, what was *that* about?

He recalled their intimate kiss a couple of

days earlier, and every cell in his body warmed to the memory. If she only knew what he was thinking.

"I said I'm ready." Her voice broke into his thoughts.

He snapped to. "Ready for what?"

"To eat." She sounded exasperated. "Oh, but first I need to burp her." She lightly massaged Tara's back while the baby lay on her stomach.

Terrance approached the isolette and peered inside. The baby had a look of bliss on her face that made both of them laugh.

"What are you serving her? Tranquilizers?"

Jaynie blinked. Her radiant smile brought a grin to his face. *Everything* she did turned him on.

"She pigged out and then passed out. I'll have to wake her up long enough to burp her, and then she'll go back to sleep."

An adult-sized belch from the newborn reverberated across the room, and set them both to giggling.

Jaynie crossed her eyes with playful embarrassment. "Well, excuse us."

Terrance caught himself grinning like a proud father. "That's our Peanut," he said. "Now, how about that lunch?"

"Sure," she said.

Now that Tara had belched, Jaynie repositioned her onto her back. She kissed two fingers and lightly touched them to Tara's forehead. "See you later, Peanut."

He looked over Jaynie's shoulder at his content daughter, catching a whiff of lavender soap in Jaynie's hair and feeling too close for comfort.

As though a bucket of cold water had been dumped on his head, he got a grip.

This can never be. I'm not part of her plan and she's not part of mine.

Backing off, he led the way to the ward door, and hardly said two words while they walked to the elevator.

CHAPTER SEVEN

ON MONDAY, Terrance showed up to help Jaynie paint her living room wall. He had a gift in tow, and held up a hand to ward off any of Jaynie's protests.

"The NICU nurses said this is the most creative bed available."

He pushed the box he held in his arms toward her, so she could read the Australian brand-name. The picture showed a bassinet-size bed hanging suspended by a spring and crossbar from a sturdy steel frame.

"They said that every time the baby moves, a gentle rocking motion lulls her back to sleep."

Jaynie started to respond, but like a salesman on a mission—a salesman in tight jeans and a black tee shirt—he continued. "And, because it's slightly upright, it will help if Tara has gastric reflux. And she'll feel more secure, cuddled in the curve of the bed, than in a large open and flat crib."

Before Jaynie could say a word, he ripped open the box and fished out the contents, then set to work putting everything together, like a dad on Christmas morning.

"It's lightweight enough to carry from room to room, so you can keep an eye on her, too."

Speechless, Jaynie watched. There would be no refusing his gift. Terrance's gesture of concern for her baby moved her more than she could admit; she shook her head in resignation.

"Why are you doing this?" She'd only meant to think the words, but they snuck out on a whisper.

Temporarily outsmarted by the metal poles, he stopped to scratch his head. He turned to her and, looking earnest as all hell, said, "Because I care."

She blinked.

Why should you care?

"Well, thank you." A wave of post-partum

nostalgia—surely that was what it was?—
threatened to overtake her. She glanced away
to toughen up. "I'm very touched."

He gazed at his feet, then back up, and whispered, "You're welcome."

Fearing she could get used to being cared
about, she let her gaze dance away. Instead, she
forced herself to calculate the steps she'd read
for painting a wall—a task she'd never done
before.

Desperate to change the feel-good mood in
the room, Jaynie spread the drop cloth on the
floor and opened the first can of paint, while
Terrance distracted himself with setting up the
bed.

"So, why are we painting that wall red?" he
asked, in a casual, more distant tone.
Apparently he'd caught her drift.

Jaynie gave the thick red liquid one last stir
with a wooden stick before stopping to answer.
"Kim's grandmother said I needed to bring
more of the five energies into my house. This
red wall will represent fire." She put her hands

on her jeans-clad hips and glanced across the room. "And I'm bringing in water energy with my indoor rock fountain. See?"

Terrance followed her hand and studied her newest purchase, bubbling and rippling over a slab of smooth black rock. He gave a nod. "Nice," he said. "Peaceful."

"And I'm bringing in earth energy with large indoor plants," she said. "Green is good." Spurred on by all the extra reading she'd done on the topic, she felt positive. "I can feel a difference already."

Clearly amused, he gave her a thumbs-up sign. And they passed the next hour side-by-side, painting in quiet, relaxed camaraderie.

In the middle of his using a roller brush to finish the last section of wall, Terrance's cellphone rang. "Can you get that for me, Jaynie?"

Her hands were free, and much cleaner than his, but she had to fish the phone from his back pocket, flip it open and place it snug against his ear—which felt far too intimate.

She tensed.

"Hello?" He looked at her and nodded his thanks. "Hey, Dave." He smiled.

Jaynie studied the tiny golden flecks in his hazel eyes while he concentrated on the conversation. Damn, he was good-looking, and it irritated the hell out of her.

"No kidding?" he said.

With new resolve, she vowed not to get sidetracked from her goal of being a mother and raising her kid…without a man. She looked away, concentrating on her feet. A paint-by-numbers kind of woman herself, who liked everything in life planned out to the tee, she'd never be compatible with a free-form action artist like Terrance, who loved extreme sports and grabbing life by the horns, going with the flow.

Why even *think* about a guy like him? She'd had her chance once, and had chosen to walk away. If she recalled correctly, he hadn't exactly come chasing after her to come back, either.

"I really appreciate it," he said. "I'm a little tight for cash right now."

She lifted her head with interest.

"Great. Later." He raised dark honey-colored eyebrows, cueing Jaynie to fold up the phone and slip it back into his pocket. She tried not to notice his high and firm rear end while she used two fingers—as if the phone had cooties—to replace it. She resisted a disturbing urge to pat his bum when she'd finished.

"Hey!" he said with a self-satisfied smile.

Her head shot up faster than a guilty pickpocket.

"Dave offered me his frequent flyer points." He finished his last stroke on the wall. "So I can fly to Massachusetts and North Carolina for my medical school interviews. As soon as I can make arrangements for time off work, I'm flying out."

"That's fantastic." She tried to sound more enthusiastic than she felt. An odd empty feeling nibbled at the pit of her stomach. Though happy for his goals and accomplishments, she had let Terrance get too close. She'd have to put an end to it right away. With new determination, she straightened her back. "I really hope your plans work out." She *did* mean it. Jaynie wanted him to be happy and successful. "I can see you as a doctor. You've got what it takes."

He grinned at her with a sparkle in his eyes, and a pleasant tickling sensation whispered across the back of her knees. Damn. Illogical as it was, she wanted to kiss him.

"Thank you for the vote of confidence. I just wish I didn't have to sell my house and move out of state in order to do it," he said, not sounding particularly enthused about the turn of events. A distant, thoughtful look passed over his face while he studied hers and ended by staring at her mouth.

Had he read her mind?

Jaynie couldn't take another second of Terrance being this close. With news of his leaving town, now was as good a time as any to start distancing herself from Terrance and the silent dreams he could never fulfill.

She went to work cleaning up, getting busy with every ridiculous detail she could think of—anything to break away from his allure.

Oh, but *he* wouldn't leave well enough alone. He reached for her arm, forcing her to look at him. Blood rushed up her neck, settling in her cheeks. A mischievous hazel glow peered at her.

"You've got paint on your face," he said.

Hands full and busy, she raised her forearm to capture the smudge, not having a clue where it was.

Terrance wiped the paint from his own hands on a rag, and stepped forward. "Let me." He helped her dispose of the paintbrush and roller bin on the tarp, and used his long, sturdy index finger to gently wipe above her upper lip. Tracing the entire length of her mouth in the same fashion, his fingertip trailed down to her chin.

Faster than she could blink, his hazel eyes turned to smoke-tinged topaz. Heat pulsed all the way to her toes, and she held her breath. He moved closer and took her face in his hands.

Before she could breathe, he covered her lips with his own. Long, sensual seconds passed, with his lush warmth teasing her mouth. She breathed with him, relaxed, and found her hands pressing the firm curves of his shoulders. And when his tongue lightly flicked hers, she clenched her fingers tight on his solid muscles. She wanted to move closer, but the hands framing her jaw and ears kept them a safe distance apart.

He was in control.

The kiss felt tender, and wonderfully woozy, and she longed for more. He angled his head to delve deeper, pressing harder with his luscious mouth and tongue.

Time stopped.

At that moment in her life, Jaynie realized that no one had ever kissed her like Terrance. Even the other night, when she'd clearly been out of her head with grief, his kiss had both stirred her up and calmed her down. She'd definitely missed his kisses since they'd broken up.

He tasted as delicious as he looked—a mixture of earthiness and the Gatorade he'd been sipping. A special blend of Terrance and aftershave invaded her nostrils and conjured memories of the last time they'd kissed.

Her knees felt like noodles.

The inviting sounds of their soulful kisses sent chills to her shoulders and breasts. Tingling, familiar tingling, circled her nipples, and she foggily realized her milk was letting down.

Oh, but she didn't want the pleasure to end.

Terrance released her face, taking time to stroke and rearrange her hair before wrapping his firm arms around her, drawing her tight to his chest. She dropped her head back so their lips could stay connected, and encircled his neck with her hands.

She'd give him whatever he wanted— anything to keep kissing him. His hips and thighs pressed flush to hers, burning through her clothes. She could feel him coming alive in his jeans, which sent an added thrill through her. Jaynie's fingers knotted into the thick, masculine hair at his nape, where, beneath, she found a strong, solid neck to knead. She massaged while he ravished her with his hot, moist mouth.

Full body chills sent her reeling. Milk-mist sprayed from her breasts, soon turning to large and constant drips. Shortly, the front of her blouse was soaked through.

He groaned.

Large hands wandered over her back, shoulders and hips while he continued to devour her mouth. He reached beneath her bottom and hoisted her tighter to him, pulling her up onto her toes. She anchored herself to his neck and chest, wrapping her thigh around his hip, molding body to body.

Their tongues searched deeply and freely, tasting and savoring each other. They breathed together, completely in sync. Her saturated shirt spilled over to his tee shirt…cold, damp… sticky.

He broke from their kiss and gave a puzzled look. Feeling chagrined, Jaynie bit her kiss-swollen lower lip, knitted her brows, and pleaded for understanding with an earnest stare.

Lust glowed in his eyes. A slow smile evolved on his face. "Can't say I've ever had this effect on a woman before."

Terrance adjusted himself in his jeans while Jaynie escaped to the bathroom to clean up. No question about it. He knew beyond a doubt that he was in lust with her. And she was the mother of his child. What a tidy little turn of events…a ready-made family of three. And what terrible timing.

Long ago he'd decided never to become a father again, had even signed up for the surgery to make sure he never would. Now, his dream of going to med school was closer than ever. And he might have to leave the state in order to follow through.

What the hell was he supposed to do?

He needed more time to think, and his leaving town would give him the perfect reason to do it.

As soon as Jaynie came back out he'd excuse himself, make plans to leave town and do battle with his conscience some other time.

* * *

The next morning, Dr. Shrinivasan's early phone call startled Jaynie. She braced herself.

"We have a good update for you on this delightful day," he said.

A quick prayer of thanks crossed her lips before she responded to his greeting. "Yes?"

"We shall send Tara home on Friday."

She couldn't believe the words. First she felt joy, and then panic set in.

My God, what do I do now?

She gave herself a pep talk. *I can do this.* Hadn't she been preparing for this moment ever since Tara had been born, one month ago?

Joy beyond all dreams circulated through her body.

My baby is coming home!

He continued. "Tara is maintaining her body temperature while in an open crib, she feeds well by mouth, and there are no recent major medical changes. I recommend that you spend the next day or two giving complete care to your baby. For best success, it is imperative that you know exactly what to expect when she comes to your home."

"Yes, of course," she agreed.

Armed with the most spectacular news of her life—aside from the day her pregnancy test had come back positive—Jaynie jumped from bed and raced to the shower.

Her only regret was that Terrance wasn't there to share it with her.

Friday came before Jaynie felt completely ready. But would she *ever* feel totally prepared for being a full-time mom? She'd spent two extensive days with the Newborn Nursery nurses, learning every trick of the trade. She'd worked from morning until night caring for Tara. She fed, diapered, bathed, managed her medication and fiddled with machinery under trained nursing supervision. And had gone home each night exhausted to her bones.

Every night during the week Jaynie had lain awake worrying, wondering how she'd rate as a true-life mother, yet eager to find out.

Kim had helped her do one last major house-clean, and given her a surprise gift of a special crib that attached directly alongside her own bed.

"This will help you sleep better, knowing Tara's right next to you." Even Kim had sounded more like an expert than Jaynie felt. "You'll have your own space, but Tara'll be within an arm's reach for nursing or anything else."

"Thank you!" Jaynie said. "You are so smart."

"Actually, my hunky pharmacist suggested it. His sister just had a baby."

Jaynie's favorite nurse had given her a few last-minute pointers about the importance of using the "sling" to keep Tara comfy and cozy beside her throughout the day.

And she'd received a crash course on handling the apnea monitor.

"Tara will have spells," one of the crusty older nurses had informed her. "The monitor will alert you to As and Bs."

"What does that mean?" Jaynie had scratched her head and felt her neck tense.

"Apnea and bradycardia. It won't sound unless she forgets to breathe for twenty seconds or if her heart-rate drops below eighty. Don't panic. Just rub her back or stimulate her to help her remember to breathe." She had glanced over the top of the gold-framed glasses perched on the tip of her nose. "The irritating sound of the monitor warning may even startle her into breathing. Look—" she'd clicked her tongue "—she has these spells several times a day. Preemies generally do. No biggie. Just keep alert…stay on top of it."

Easy for her to say. Her nursing shift ended after eight hours. Jaynie's heart had galloped, and a wave of concern had circled her head.

I can do this. I'm a nurse. Heck, I'm a mother!

They'd also given her a crash course on infant CPR. Sure, she'd practiced annually at work, on unnaturally pink plastic infant dummies. She'd covered the stiff doll's nose and mouth with her own to puff air inside, and had used two fingers between the nipples to quickly beat out the required compressions, but that was pretend.

Before her lay her daughter, the most precious gift she'd ever been given, and Jaynie didn't want to botch anything up.

Tara had flourished in the past few weeks to a whopping 1700 grams—just a few ounces short of the four-pound goal. But when Jaynie carried her to the car on the day of discharge, Tara felt as fragile as a tiny antique treasure. Jaynie had held her breath when she'd lifted her from the hospital isolette, and when Tara had squirmed and mewed, she'd looked on with both wonder and love.

Kim and her boyfriend, Dr. Tommy Tom, had offered to bring Jaynie and Tara home. She had eagerly accepted. Even Por Por Chang had sent over some food guaranteed to increase her milk and give her added energy.

Though the food looked and smelled weird, it meant the world to Jaynie, since her own mother couldn't make the trip out west for a few more weeks.

It took three adult minds and twenty minutes to figure out the placement of the car seat in back of Jaynie's SUV, but they prevailed. And when they arrived home, other than holding Tara, Jaynie left Kim and Tommy to carry everything else inside.

"Put that over there," Kim said when they entered the house. She had gotten very good at bossing Tommy around.

The tall man sported broad shoulders under a peach-colored J. Crew shirt, and a trendy ultra-short haircut, gelled and spiked to perfection. His tiny dark eyes sparkled when he looked at Kim, and it made Jaynie smile.

The look of love.

He unloaded several bundles of items Jaynie and Kim had deemed necessary for Tara: car seat, diaper bag, apnea monitor, pulmonary treatment machine, nursing supplies, another bag of medicine and supplementary formula. He made two trips to the car to bring everything inside.

Over the next hour, the three of them bustled around, setting everything up according to Jaynie's need and desire.

Kim finally whisked her waist-length hair behind her shoulders, placed her hands on her narrow hips and gave the nursery the once-over. "Anything you need?"

Jaynie scanned the room and shook her head. She'd slipped Tara into a sling and snuggled her close to her breasts. The baby looked peaceful and content, and Jaynie's confidence grew. "No. I should be fine…really."

After wavering for several seconds, Kim hugged Jaynie, took Tommy by the arm and headed for the door. "Don't hesitate to call for anything, okay?"

When the door closed, Jaynie was surprised by the strong sense of isolation that settled in around her.

The house was dead quiet.

Tara remained asleep, and Jaynie felt exhausted. She decided to take advantage and put her feet up for a few minutes—maybe even take a catnap. She gingerly angled herself onto the couch and rested her head against the cushion. She repositioned Tara in the sling onto her abdomen. Jaynie's eyes felt heavy and she welcomed the sluggish feeling lulling her toward sleep. Ah…rest.

A sharp, fussy cry came from the vicinity of her chest. With her brain swimming back from its stupor, Jaynie's head shot up. Tara had a healthy pair of lungs on her, and, judging by the foul smell wafting through the air, was in need of a diaper change.

By Sunday night, Jaynie hadn't gotten more than one and a half hours' consecutive sleep at any given time. What was left of her stored energy had evaporated by Saturday morning, and she'd been dragging through the last two days. Deep blue circles under her eyes made her complexion look pasty. Even her normally curly hair looked droopy and dull, and her brown eyes had turned lifeless.

She'd lied to anyone who'd called to check

in and see how she was doing. She'd told every single one of her friends from work, her mother, Kim and even Dr. Shrinivasan, that everything was hunky-dory, she couldn't be happier, all was well.

Secretly, she felt irritated that Terrance hadn't called her once while he'd been gone. But what was the point? So they'd kissed a couple times. He wasn't part of her life anymore than she or Tara were part of his.

Exhausted, she wanted to cry. Of course she loved her baby. Jaynie loved every second of caring for Tara's multiple needs: listening for her to breathe whenever she lay down to rest; nursing every two hours on the dot; bathing her; changing her diapers; giving her breathing treatments. On and on and on.

But over the last seventy-two hours the feather-light bundle constantly attached to her chest while awake, had begun to feel like a brick. Jaynie could hardly hold her own head up, let alone shoulder the full responsibility of caring for Tara.

She knew she needed to eat, but was too tired to care for herself, too. She'd skipped bathing altogether on Sunday, opting for precious moments of shut-eye whenever Tara napped. Her nerves twinged raw, she felt edgy, lethargic and sad.

Carefully placing the bedside intercom next to Tara's crib in the nursery, after lying her on her back, she checked for a third time to make sure the apnea monitor leads were properly attached to her chest. Countless false alarms had fired over the weekend, keeping her on edge and running for the crib due to loose leads. Determined to take a shower during this naptime, she checked them once again.

Jaynie set up the other walkie-talkie monitor on the bathroom counter and switched it on. A static swishing sound reported the humming of the humidifier and total silence from Tara's bed.

Stripping naked, she changed her mind and ran a tub full of hot water for a bath. Jaynie was shocked when she looked at herself in the mirror. She was now gaunt and flagging, and the glow of pregnancy had disappeared, replaced with exhaustion and depression. Not a glamorous combination.

She dipped her toe into the invitingly warm water in the tub and prepared to slip inside for a few moments of paradise. The loud buzzing of the apnea monitor sounded its alarm. Jaynie reached for her bathrobe and threw it on while rushing to Tara's side. After tying her sash, she found Tara peacefully sleeping, with one monitor lead dangling from beneath her cotton drawstring gown.

She carefully reapplied the lead to her tummy, praying she wouldn't wake or disturb her baby. Checking one last time, to make sure all the leads were in place, and the tiny oxygen cannula was set properly inside each nostril, Jaynie retreated.

Walking like a zombie, she found herself in the dining room, weak and leaning against the wall for support. Dismay, melancholy, intense fatigue and a total sense of defeat mixed into a dangerous brew of hopelessness.

Finally coming undone, she felt tears fill her eyes. She slid down the wall to the hardwood floor, where she crumpled into a fetal position and let out a total melt-down wail.

CHAPTER EIGHT

WHERE was Tara? Standing in the newborn ward, Terrance fought off a burst of alarm and searched for one of the nurses. He'd returned home late Friday night, and to make up for taking extra days off had worked a double shift on Saturday. Now, Sunday afternoon, he'd finally found time to visit Peanut. But where was she?

He hurried toward a nurse changing a diaper. A look of recognition crossed her face when she glanced up.

"Where's Tara?"

"Went home Friday morning," the curt older nurse said over her shoulder.

A crushing sense of loss hit him in the chest. He'd made up his mind about Jaynie and Tara.

He'd searched his soul—even had a long talk with Dave—and was anxious to follow through on his plans. Now was as good a time as any, but he'd have to wait until he got off work.

Though still daylight, the shadowy late May afternoon made the house look dark from the porch. Terrance tapped on the door, but Jaynie didn't answer. He cupped his hands to his eyes and peered through the front window.

"Jaynie?" he called.

Nothing.

He caught a glimpse of someone's feet on the dining room floor. Fear shot through his chest, and he dashed for the door and jangled the handle, surprised to find the latch not securely locked. With a little finessing, he got it open. It squeaked against the silence.

A cold chill ran the course of his spine.

Oh, God, what could have happened here?

Rushing through the door, he flipped on a light switch and found Jaynie on the floor, curled up and whimpering. Where was Tara?

He sprinted to the nursery and found her peacefully asleep. Terrance dashed back to Jaynie's side and dropped to his knees.

"Jaynie? What's wrong?"

She stirred. "Go away."

He brushed the hair back from her face. Resembling a wild street urchin, Jaynie blinked and squinted at him.

"Are you sick?"

"I'm fine," she croaked. "Leave me alone."

"Like hell you are." He scooped his hands beneath her, lifted her up and carried her toward the bedroom. "You look like you haven't slept all week." He laid her down on the bed and carefully tightened the sash on her robe, then tucked her beneath the covers. "Sleep," he said. "I'll take care of everything else."

Jaynie attempted to sit up and climb out, but he gently pushed her back toward the pillow. "Stay right where you are. I'm not kidding, lady. You need to sleep."

"But...the baby..."

"But nothing. I'll take care of the baby. Go

to sleep. That's an order." He clicked off the lamp and tiptoed out, shutting the door behind him.

Jaynie woke up in a pitch-black room. She glanced at the red digital numbers on her clock: 7:00. Nighttime? She shot upright, realizing her nursing schedule was way off. Her breasts felt heavy and tight.

"Oh, my God. *Tara.*"

She lunged for the door and flung it open, certain her baby had died from neglect. The rest of the house was lit up. She raced to the nursery and found it empty. Fear shocked her like a thrown bucket of cold water. She sped to the dining room and whirled toward the living room.

Terrance sat reading the newspaper while Tara dozed contentedly nearby, in the hanging bassinette. He looked up and furrowed his brow. "Go back to bed."

A warm, calming wave overlapped her terror. She shook her head and fought to take back control.

"I need to feed her."

He made a big to-do about folding up the paper and putting it down. With hands on his knees, he said, "Go back to bed." He glanced at Tara and back. "As soon as she wakes up, I'll bring her to you." Pointing to the door, he re-iterated, "Go."

Over two hours had passed since she'd slipped into oblivion. Wasn't Tara starving? Jaynie had to admit her baby looked quite comfy in the unique hammock-style bed. But knowing well Tara's routine, Jaynie was assured that she would scream her lungs out when she was hungry—just like she'd done all weekend.

Nodding her head, deciding she could wait a little longer before feeding time, Jaynie somberly returned to her room. She slumped down onto her bed and nestled back for more rest. She knew she needed it. Any "new parent" reference book in her library would tell her to get plenty of sleep. A yawn escaped her lips. Following the lure of her pillow, she quickly dozed off.

A gentle tugging on her shoulder drew her

back to the world of the living. Terrance towered above her, tall and handsome in the dim light. He extended Tara, all bundled up and fussing, towards her.

The clock read 8:00.

"She's hungry," he whispered, in a ragged yet gentle voice.

Jaynie sat up, reached for her baby, and positioned her in the crook of her arm. She glanced toward Terrance; ever the gentleman he'd turned his back. She offered Tara her breast and contented suckling noises soon filled the otherwise quiet room.

He walked to the window and gazed outside, but he didn't break the silence. He peered through the blinds, cleared his throat, shifted back and forth on his heels and the balls of his feet, even fiddled with the change in his pockets. But he never said a word. After a while, he sat on the lone chair in the room, closed his eyes and leaned back, lacing his fingers behind his head. She smiled at his composure.

When she'd finished nursing Tara, Jaynie

cleared her throat, alerting him, and he dutifully retrieved her.

"I'll take over from here," he said. "Go back to sleep."

Woozy from the pleasure of nursing, and craving more rest, Jaynie couldn't bring herself to protest. She rolled onto her side and nestled into her pillow. Eyes heavy with slumber, a contented smile on her face, she forced herself to speak. "Don't forget to burp Tara and change her dia…"

The door closed.

Every two to three hours throughout the night Terrance brought Tara to Jaynie. Repeating the routine, she nursed the baby and handed her back, falling immediately to sleep. And finally, by morning light, she woke up feeling human again. She stretched, lazily yawned, and climbed out of bed, heading for the shower.

First she wandered down the hall, peeked around the corner into the living room, and found Terrance sprawled on the couch, slack-jawed and out to the world. She smiled at the sight. Tara was nearby in her portable bed. Both were breathing, and she didn't smell any evidence of dirty diapers, so Jaynie went contentedly off to bathe.

Terrance walked into the kitchen, scratching his stomach and yawning. A promise of fresh-brewed coffee beckoned. Jaynie stood at the counter in loose fitting sports pants and a snug white polo shirt, looking slimmer than he'd remembered before his trip. Her hair, fresh from the shower, hung in damp ringlets to her shoulders. Even without a stitch of make-up on, she held his immediate and undivided attention.

"Good morning," she said, looking shy and squeaky-clean.

"Good morning." He squeezed her arm on his way to the percolator, unable to decide which smelled better—Jaynie or the coffee. He liked how the natural-as-living greeting felt. He'd have liked it even more if they'd shared the same bed last night.

"Don't you have to go to work?"

She broke into his thoughts while he poured himself a cup. "I worked the weekend and I've got today off."

He took a long satisfying sip, made the requisite "ahh" sound, and grinned. "Don't even think about getting rid of me. I'm sticking around. You need me."

In place of the protest he expected, a smile broke across her face. But she recovered quickly, leaned against the counter, crossed her arms and watched him, attempting to look stern with giveaway eyes.

Terrance fought the urge to fold her into an embrace, bury his nose in her jasmine-scented hair and kiss her neck until she ripped off his clothes. Instead, he made a nervy, lopsided smirk, daring her to resist him.

"Well," she said. "In that case, the least I can do is make you breakfast."

Jaynie had offered her bathroom so Terrance could take a quick shower after they ate. Later, they both found themselves standing before the same sink with Tara's plastic bathtub, filling it with warm water. She pondered his intense interest in her child's care. What was that all about?

"Let me do it," he said, and he moved closer to the vanity. His big hand held over half of Tara's entire body. The infant squirmed and drew her tiny legs up tight to her pink tummy, and then widened her eyes and pushed the tip of her minuscule tongue to her lips in surprise. One little peep escaped her mouth when he submerged the lower part of her body into the water. After tensing, her scrawny legs relaxed, until she cooed and gurgled.

Tara liked her bath.

Jaynie laughed at the look of clear amazement in Terrance's eyes. "See—it's fun." She giggled. "I told you."

The smile he gave almost knocked her flip-flops off her feet. And, oh, what a fine profile the man had when he turned back to finish his assigned job of bathing a four-pound infant.

Jaynie had never imagined the smell of baby lotion and natural male could be such an aphrodisiac.

She was puzzled. Either he was a natural at bathing a baby, or he'd done it before. Why did he want to help her? And, more importantly, why did she trust him so much? He'd been a godsend last night, and she'd never forget how he'd come to her rescue. But why choose to stick around today?

After the bath, she helped Terrance swathe Tara in a towel and gently dried the beginnings of the fine, red-tinged hair on her head. Tara griped and squirmed.

Jaynie and Terrance looked at each other and gave happy-face smiles over the wonder of it all. And something more, something intense, even urgent, passed between them.

"So, you want to tell me what happened over the weekend?" he asked, while putting a new diaper on Tara like a pro.

Jaynie sighed and leaned against the counter. "I felt completely overwhelmed—all the equipment, and Tara's treatments, not to mention nursing her every two hours—I never got to sleep." She closed her eyes and tried to block the horrible feeling of failure from her mind. "It just all caught up with me."

"Why didn't you ask for help?"

She rolled her eyes. "Stubborn. Foolish, I guess. Shouldn't I be able to handle all of this myself?"

"Nope." Terrance attempted to wrap Tara in a light blanket.

Jaynie stepped in and demonstrated the swaddling technique.

"I can't thank you enough." She touched his arm and reacted in her gut. "I don't know what I would have done if you hadn't come."

He held Tara like a football in the bend of his arm. "You'd have pulled yourself together and called someone. That much I know."

He had faith in her.

His eyes wandered to her face, and she flushed warm when she saw the same look he'd given her the other day, just after their kiss.

"Whew, it's steamy in here." She tore away from his intense gaze and opened the bathroom door, breaking the moment and escaping his sensual spell.

Over the next several hours they diapered, fed, medicated and spent an inordinate amount of time just watching Tara. Any and every little thing she did tickled them. Her belches were hysterical, and the look she gave just before pooping had them in stitches. The zapped look of contentment on her face after nursing made them both coo. And when she gurgled? Well, what could they do but beam with pride?

Terrance made sure Jaynie napped regularly and ate properly throughout the day. He also swept the floors, did her laundry, straightened up the house and ran to the market for groceries. At nine o'clock that night, he escorted Jaynie to bed, made her promise she'd call him if she had any problems, and assured her he'd be back the next day, after work.

She plopped into bed, with Tara nearby in the

attached bedside crib, and securely connected her to the apnea monitor. The wonderful day had come to an end. And the icing on the cake had been a tender goodnight kiss from her new hero—Terrance. It might have seemed casual to him—his leaning down and gently pressing his lips to her forehead—but to Jaynie it had felt like the kiss of a prince.

A prince who had tiptoed out of the room and shut the door.

The last thought on Jaynie's mind before she drifted off to sleep was how wonderful it was to have someone…

Tuesday morning, Terrance had just finished making work assignments when his beeper went off. He recognized the number as the emergency room. Knowing they'd have whatever equipment he'd need, he rushed to the stairwell, avoiding the notoriously slow hospital elevators, navigating his way to the ER.

He punched in the code numbers to enter the locked ward and swept through the doors toward the nurses' station. Through the over-crowded bustle and noise, the charge nurse alerted him to the incoming ambulance and its estimated time of arrival.

"SIDS," she said casually, as if it happened every day of the week.

Terrance's heart stopped. *What if it was Tara?* All reason about the statistical odds of it actually being his daughter left his head. His normally steady-as-steel hands trembled like leaves on a windy day. He shook his head to help re-focus his vision.

How would he be of any use to the code team, falling apart like this?

"Are you okay?" The charge nurse had picked up on the fact that all the blood had drained from his face.

He couldn't bring himself to answer and fumbled for a chair to sit down. She approached him, waving something she'd pulled from her pocket.

The potent ammonia ampule she'd popped open under his nose burned his lungs, forced his attention, and started him breathing again. He swatted her hand away.

"Just tell me where the baby is coming from, how old it is and is it anyone we know?"

"The paramedics said it's a two-month-old boy. And he's not dead, but he's gone into cardiac arrest."

The emotional whirlwind blew out of his mind. Relieved beyond belief, Terrance gathered his composure, quit thinking like a father and started thinking like an unflappable respiratory therapist.

He prepared for a battle of life and death, determined along with the rest of the code team to make sure the baby boy had a fighting chance to see his first birthday.

And once he'd made sure the child was stable, first chance he got, he'd call Jaynie and ask how Tara was doing today.

The last ten days had passed beautifully with Terrance's help. Jaynie mused what a blessing he'd been on the way home from her six-week post-partum checkup. She had trusted him to babysit while she went, and there were no messages on her cellphone, which was a good sign.

Pulling her car into the driveway, she was delightfully surprised to see Terrance looking huge, and Tara microscopic, on the front porch. He waved at her with a broad smile. All was well.

She parked and he greeted her on the steps with a kiss on the cheek. Jaynie was in love with him. She couldn't deny it. But she'd keep her secret for now, and most likely for always. By the dreamy look on his face, she guessed he might have feelings for her, too. She knew what she wished for—now, if she could only read his mind…

"So, how'd it go?" he asked, handing a squirming Tara to her.

"The good news is I'm doing great," she said, reaching for her baby and making little cooing sounds of comfort and clicks of her tongue. She looked up and grew serious. "The bad news is that means I've got to go back to work in a week."

"Do you feel ready for that?" He raised a brow.

"I'm not sure." She patted Tara's back.

"What about Peanut?"

"I've made arrangements with one of the retired NICU nurses to watch her while I work, and then my mom will be here for a couple of weeks."

Terrance looked as if he wanted to ask more, but refrained. He opened the door and followed her inside.

"Oh, yeah. She's ready to eat," he said.

Jaynie gave a salute. "Reporting for duty, sir." She smiled and gurgled at Tara, and carried her into the nursery to feed and put her down, then closed the door.

Tara liked a long nap in the afternoons, and Jaynie looked forward to some time alone with Terrance. They had grown closer over the last month. Closer than she'd ever been with her ex-boyfriend over the five years they were together—which was rather amazing, considering she had wanted to marry that jerk. And definitely closer than when she and Terrance had dated last year. What had brought about this change? Was it Tara?

She intended to explore her perplexing feelings for Terrance more, but not right now. Her mind was on something else—something big and gorgeous to look at.

Terrance had been evasive whenever she'd brought up his medical school interviews. "Things went great," he'd say, or, "I'll see whether they accept me or not and go from there." But he'd never go into particulars.

Astounded by the depth of her newfound love for Terrance, Jaynie feared the day he would quit Mercy Hospital and march off to another university across the country, leaving her and Tara with a huge gap to fill.

For the first time in her life she wanted to risk it all—give her soul, have her heart ripped from her chest or spend the rest of her life alone—for even one moment of paradise with

Terrance. No book could tell her how to go about it; she'd have to write this one herself.

So, after her thorough checkup, and at her own request, Dr. Marks had fit Jaynie for a diaphragm. And now, this very afternoon, she had high hopes of getting to use it. After all he'd done for her, Terrance had some serious "thank-you" sex due him. Not that he'd think of it that way. But she was looking for an excuse—any excuse—to make love to him. Her fantasy mission was to spend the afternoon close to him, in his arms.

Under Terrance's tender loving care and feeding, she felt like a new woman. So, after putting Tara to nap, filled with determination, energy and lust for life—lust for Terrance, anyway—Jaynie closed the nursery door and sauntered into the living room.

He sat in the rocking chair, looking like Adonis, reading the paper. Sunlight shimmered through the shoulder-length hair that framed his face. Her mouth went dry.

"I'm going to get something to drink," she said. "Would you like anything?"

"Sure. Water." He smiled appreciatively.

Her legs *felt* like water. She needed to regroup, gather more confidence. Positive that she hadn't been misreading the multitude of signals he'd given her, she filled one glass, took a few swallows, filled another and headed back to the living room, all the while doing battle with her nerves. Why hadn't she thought to read a book about seducing the man of your dreams?

She brought the water and handed it to him, then circled behind the chair and placed her hands on his wide shoulders. She began to gently massage with warm, vigorous strokes. She admired his strength. He groaned and put down the water. His head fell forward in apparent bliss for a few moments before he straightened.

"Come here," he said, and reached behind for Jaynie's hand. "Sit on my lap."

Taking a subtle deep breath, she complied, sitting sideways across his thighs. He gazed at her and smiled—there was that look again— and a flock of butterflies flew into her chest.

Go for it.

She put her arms around his neck and nuzzled his cheek. Fine stubble tickled her, awakening nerve-endings she hadn't even known she had. Could the jaw be an erogenous zone?

His large, warm hand caressed her face and she felt his heart thump in his chest. Terrance turned his head and kissed her, long and hard, building their passion slowly. He pulled back just enough to speak.

"I think that red-hot Feng Shui wall is working wonders on the energy in this room."

She broke away and gazed into his eyes. "You may be right. But I don't want to think about anything right now." Her body softened, melting onto his, while their mouths greeted each other again. He probed with his tongue, playful and adventurous, steadily building, firmer and stronger, until the kiss became urgent, desperate. His hands moved over her back, rubbing, kneading and drawing her tight to his body.

On a whim, and fueled by their kiss, she shifted her position, swinging her leg over his lap, facing him full-on. She took his face into her hands and kissed him the way she'd dreamed about over the past week. He moaned and gave himself to her, boosting her confidence. She felt his response under her thigh and grew even braver, pressing into it in a full straddle. A surge of sensation coursed through her core and a new boldness emerged. She'd take control and run with it.

His hands shot to the small of her back and pulled her forward. He pressed her firmly against his arousal, pleasuring and taunting them both.

She moaned. "More. I want more."

He groaned.

Jaynie broke from his kiss and dropped her head back. Following her hint, he kissed her neck, licking the skin, drawing it into his mouth. She purred and subtly rocked back and forth with their hips locked in place. It felt too good. Heavenly was more like it.

"You're driving me crazy." His voice brought her back from wicked, wonderful mindlessness.

Seeing dazed desire in his eyes, she silently got up and with a trembling hand took his, then led him down the hall…into her room.

The bed called out—large, cool and empty.

Terrance had an impulse to grab Jaynie and throw her onto the mattress and ravish her. Instead, practicing self-restraint, he fumbled and unbuttoned her blouse, all the while frantically feathering kisses lightly across her neck and chest. God, he loved how she responded with shivers. The last button was stubborn, and he popped it open like a snap—hoped she didn't mind. By the intense look on her face, she didn't seem to. His excitement grew when he unveiled her lace bra and the lovely flesh hiding just beneath. His fingers explored the bra in total concentration and awe, then boldly removed it.

"So beautiful," he said.

Her breath caught when he leaned forward

and kissed her breasts, gently cupping each one before pressing firmly, memorizing the feel. His thumb lightly swept each nipple until it pebbled. He pulled his head back, to better admire her, and loved what he saw.

Anxious to be skin to skin, he didn't bother to unbutton his shirt, but ripped it open, sending buttons flying around the room. He laughed as he stripped it off, and she did, too. It helped him relax and calm down the tiniest bit.

Aching with desire, he clutched her bare back, holding her tight, caressing the heat of her skin in his palms, amazed by her silky, soft feel.

They finished undressing each other in a frenzied fashion, unzipping, tugging, removing the final barriers. Finally naked, they embraced.

The thrill was more than Jaynie could bear. Discovering a glorious new joy of touch, she closed her eyes and, with eager hands, savored every centimeter of skin, muscle and sinew on his body.

He lowered himself onto the bed and reached for her. She crawled on top, sharing her breasts, hips and stomach with his flesh. Heat flashed up her body, flaming her desire. His breathing grew rough when he enfolded her in his arms. Inhaling his scent, she kissed him, tasted him, loved him.

He rolled her onto her back, kissing her neck and jaw, cupping her breast and nuzzling her hair with his nose.

"You're beautiful," he said, then sat up and praised her with his eyes.

He gave her the distinct impression that at that moment in time she was the most beautiful woman in the world. Jaynie basked in his attention.

He took her peaked breast into his mouth, and a feeling completely different from her motherly role roiled through her. She arched her back and bit her lip to keep from calling out. His hand wandered across her belly and between her legs. She relaxed for him and he gently opened her, stirring new sensations. Seeming intent on giving her pleasure before taking his own, he continued with the gentle massage. She grew weak and tense at the same time. All the while he watched her, and she tried to look back, but could only concentrate on his intimate touch—until she couldn't take any more. A deep wave of release crested and rolled over her, reaching every cell in her body. When she recovered, she wanted only one thing.

"I need you," she said.

His hot hazel eyes blazed with anticipation, and then regret. "I don't have a condom."

Jaynie smiled wisely. "I stopped at the pharmacy on my way home today."

He gave a wicked grin and raised an eyebrow. "You did?" The fire in his eyes made her face flare with heat. "Great."

He latched onto her other breast with renewed vigor, taking it into his mouth, once again driving her mad.

She moaned as her hand reached for the bedside drawer, pulling it open and blindly digging through it, quickly finding the small foil packages. Never once did she think about her new diaphragm. It would mean she'd have to leave him for a minute, and she couldn't bear the thought.

He snatched a packet like lightning, fidgeted with it until it ripped open, then rolled the condom in place. Pressing her legs wider, he lunged. Then, as though remembering she'd only given birth six weeks ago, he came to an abrupt stop.

"I'm sorry." He massaged her thigh. "I want you so much, I'm having trouble controlling myself."

She smiled at his consideration, but longed for the passion in his eyes and the feel of his strong body as close as only making love allowed. Jaynie bucked her hips in answer.

"You're killing me, Jaynie."

With obvious restraint, in a long, luxuriating move, he entered, pressing slowly and completely into her, then growled.

She tensed with tenderness, but gradually yielded around his form. They met at a private, primitive place and held each other danger-ously close to the edge. He moved deeper, in and out, then deeper still, finding a perfect spot to love. Time was suspended in sensual oblivion. Step by step, she let go, losing control until she was completely his. She captured him with her hips, loving him back, asking for more, driving him deeper. Driving herself crazy.

Sweat beaded on his smooth muscled chest and she savored the salty taste, loving the hot, damp feel of him on top of her. Heat and juices mixed, making a heady scent, sending primal messages to her core.

Hovering above her, he stared into her face. She was so gone with sensation, she could barely look back. When she did, she saw raw desire burning in his eyes. He was right there with her, teetering on the edge of bliss, as close as two people could ever be.

He held her hips and tilted her just so, as if it could feel any more perfect—it did. She knotted her legs around his waist and went swimming through time and space, flying out of control on an exquisite adventure with Terrance. She rode the wave of pleasure, praying it would never end, until an apex of spasms slammed her through the other side of heaven. Jaynie gasped with intense shudders…and Terrance quickly followed.

Breathless, he collapsed beside her, seeming sated and slack with exhaustion, staying tangled and twisted with her body. He kissed her forehead and whispered, "I love you." He snuggled into her neck, and then he went still.

I love you?

Though limp, and consumed by their love-making, Jaynie shot up, ecstatic. "You do?"

He pulled her back down to his embrace. Grinning, and offering gentle kisses all over her face, he said, "Oh, yeah."

Elated, she relaxed into his arms and sighed. "I love you, too."

The perfect moment stretched into several minutes of joy and peace. Completely together. In love. Totally and monumentally content.

She drifted toward sleep.

"Are you awake?" he asked.

"Mmm…"

"I have a question." He rolled off, onto his side, and leaned on his elbow. "Who is Tara's father, Jaynie?"

She studied his face—perfection. A foreign tense feeling formed in her stomach. "A man who was never meant to be a part of my life, but who had everything to do with my future. No one you'd know."

"A one-night stand?"

"A sperm bank donor."

Obviously grappling with her answer, he furrowed his brow. "How did you choose?"

Folding her hands across her stomach, Jaynie stared at the ceiling. Thinking back, she remembered contemplating that the sperm donor's thoroughly described physical characteristics reminded her of a certain hunky respiratory therapist, at the time.

"Aside from the great vital statistics, you mean?" She grinned, trying to lighten up, but realized he was dead serious and switched tack. "If you want the truth, it came down to a picture of a boy and his sister, and a wonderful essay." She eased into a smile, remembering the moment she'd made the decision that had changed her life forever. "That clinched it for me."

His hand covered hers. "You know that my sister's name is Tara, don't you?"

"Yes," she said, and an uneasy feeling developed in her chest. "Isn't that an odd coincidence?"

"I was born with polydactyly, too."

Desperate to turn his logic into joking, she said, "Oh, and you probably give regularly to the local sperm bank—right?"

"Dave Martinez is my best friend. He's the head of the cryobank."

Jaynie's mind shot nervously to remember Dave with the shaved head. He'd helped her make the biggest decision of her life. "But it's all confidential. He had no influence over my choice."

"And he never told me a word about you."

Desperate to not make it so, she said, "It's just a coincidence…"

Terrance cleared his throat and began to recite. "'…if, in the end, I've done anything worthwhile with my life, nothing will compare to this…'"

What was he trying to tell her? She couldn't hear this—not now. "You've seen that on Tara's wall, that's all."

He sat up, reached for her hand. "I wrote it."

She pulled hers away. "It's not you."

"I gave the cryobank a picture of me and my twin sister for the package. You must have that, too."

She rolled away from him. "No."

But he wouldn't stop. He wouldn't give up. He had to torture her by driving his point home. He swept the hair from her shoulder and kissed the curve of her back.

She froze.

"I donated to that sperm bank, Jaynie…"

A vise strangled her chest. She turned to face him. "No!"

He grabbed her arms and squeezed tight, forcing her to look at him. Fire glared in his eyes. "I'm Tara's father. I'm sure of it."

"You can't be." She clenched her eyes closed and shook her head back and forth. "No!"

Her gaze darted nervously around the room, adding things up in her mind.

"Then that means you only came around because you thought you were her father."

"That's not true!"

"How else would you explain it, Terrance? We'd said goodbye before I got pregnant."

She'd been completely duped by him and his scheme to weasel into Tara's life. The child she'd planned to keep only to herself had a flesh-and-blood father. Right before her. Never again would she be content to imagine a vial with "Donor #683" marked on it, and feel safe that Tara was all hers. He'd ruined everything.

Two words formed in her throat.

"Get out!"

CHAPTER NINE

"GET out!" she repeated.

Terrance stood, looking dumbstruck.

Jaynie shouted, "Leave!" Dead serious, she bundled his clothes and threw them at him. "Now!"

"Listen to me, Jaynie…" He fumbled for his jeans.

Like a child, she cupped her hands over her ears. "I know all I need to know. How *could* you?"

He hopped on one leg, slipping the other into his pants. "I never meant to find out. Things just kept adding up."

Her gut twisted so tight, she wanted to throw up. She bit back the sting of tears, refusing to give him the satisfaction of crying. "What a fool I was. To think you were actually interested in *me*." A wry laugh escaped her lips.

His bare chest showed through the shirt without buttons. "I love you. Damn it! I wasn't lying."

He tried to grasp her arms. Confused and furious, she shrugged away.

Tara woke up crying.

Screaming.

Jaynie pushed past Terrance. "Get out," she reiterated, and stormed through the bedroom door.

He followed her. The baby's shrieks grew louder. Jaynie turned on him. "Leave us alone." She flung her hand toward the nursery and the wailing within. "Don't you see what you're doing to us?"

She saw a horrified look cross his face, and then resignation.

"This isn't over," he said, retreating back.

"Oh, yes, it is!" She practically ripped the nursery door off its hinges and rushed to Tara's crib. Forcing herself to calm down for the baby's sake, Jaynie took a deep breath—and heard the front door slam.

Only then did she let her tears flow.

Now, for the first time since she'd started nursing, she had trouble letting down her milk. Her body trembled with anger.

"How could he?" she muttered to Tara.

What kind of twisted sense of obligation did he have, to have wooed and conquered her just because he'd figured out he was the sperm donor for her baby?

"You're my baby. *My* baby." She gritted her teeth and wondered where her milk had disappeared. "He has no legal hold on you."

Tara's eyes watched her earnestly.

Jaynie had studied the cryobank contract, and several other law books she'd checked out on the subject. She *knew* he had no legal recourse.

Tara fidgeted, seeming as agitated as Jaynie felt. Things had changed from wonderful to a nightmare, all in a matter of seconds. Working to calm herself and Tara down, Jaynie forced herself to relax. She repositioned Tara in her arms and finally felt her milk let down.

With a soft, desperate whisper, she searched

her daughter's eyes and asked, "Why did I have to go and fall in love with him?"

Terrance couldn't believe what had just happened. He'd told her he loved her and she'd kicked him out. He'd consented and left—only because he'd needed time to regroup.

How had everything backfired so horribly? They had connected, he and Jaynie; they rode the same wavelength in so many ways. She was a great woman, a fantastic mother, and, oh, my God, a lover beyond all others.

Astounding.

Talk about connecting. They'd been so totally in the moment with each other back there it had scared him at first. But only for a moment. Once he'd gotten over the shock of being exactly where he'd wanted to be with her, he'd recognized the look in her eyes. They knew each other; they were meant to be together.

And his plans never to be a dad again? Shot to hell.

Now bile reared in his stomach and acid in his

throat. He loved Jaynie, and thought she loved him, too, but she'd just kicked him out of her house and her bed as if he was the world's biggest louse. He had to get things straightened out.

Pushing the pedal to the metal on his hybrid car, he almost hit sixty on the 5 Freeway heading for Silver Lake.

Now what?

Aside from Jaynie, there was only one other person Terrance wanted to talk to.

"Wow. What happened to you?" His sister, Tara, answered the door in jeans and a sweatshirt, her hair in a thick red braid.

"I just had my heart ripped out and stomped on. That's what." Terrance entered the familiar home of his twin.

A mischievous smile crossed her lips. "Ah…finally the tables have turned."

"I'm serious. I'm in love."

He plopped down onto her rattan settee and scrubbed his hands across his face. "I need a beer."

Normally, he'd have expected Tara to tell him to get it himself. But she must have seen the desperation on his face, and she left the room, heading for the kitchen without a single snide remark.

Tara returned, looking curious, with a can for him and a bottle of water for herself. Sitting across from him, yoga-style on a roomy chair, she settled in.

"Haven't I been telling you for years that when it comes to women, persistence pays off?"

He nodded, feeling a little queasy and defeated.

Her sympathetic hazel-green eyes waited expectantly. "Why don't you tell me all about it?"

He took a swig of beer, cleared his throat and began…

The phone rang again. Jaynie ignored it—again. How many times could a person call without giving up? For two days straight the phone had rung every hour between five and nine p.m. She knew it was Terrance because those were the hours after he got off work. And even now he was considerate of her need for rest by stopping the phone calls at nine.

If he'd worked last weekend, she knew he'd have this weekend off. Jaynie prayed he had some big plans to keep him away from her—like studying for term finals or a camping trip with Dave.

Every day that passed she felt herself grow weaker. She simply couldn't face the fact that she loved him with all of her heart. It wasn't part of her plan.

And he'd deceived her. It wasn't really *her* he was interested in. How could she ever forgive him?

Jaynie picked up the phone to call Kim for some distraction. On the fifth ring, when Kim picked up, she realized she'd interrupted something.

"Hello?" Kim answered, breathless.

"Hey, it's me."

Jaynie heard sheets and blankets rustling, and muffled sounds in the background.

Kim giggled. "Stop that," she said, just before putting her hand over the receiver. A moment passed. "I'm sorry, Jaynie, you caught me at a bad time."

"I'll call back later."

"No! I want to talk to you, really."

"Call me when you're, uh…er…done." Jaynie smiled for her friend, remembering her own afternoon tryst with Terrance, not so long ago, and hung up.

"I know!" Jaynie made a silly face at Tara, who was dangling in the snuggly sling on her chest, as if the baby understood everything she said. "I'll call Mrs. Bouchet. Remember her? Your future nanny?" She crossed her eyes and cooed at her daughter, who gurgled and squirmed.

"I'll ask her to come over and walk through your routine again." She strode toward the phone with added purpose. "And then I'll feed you some lunch, okay?"

Jaynie dreaded going back to work and leaving her baby in someone else's care. The only other person she trusted more than herself to care for Tara was Terrance.

In a perfect world.

But, being a single mother, Jaynie knew she had to make a living. She'd stocked up on freezing her breast milk for the past two weeks. Mrs. Bouchet, aside from being an ex-nurse, was both a mother and a grandmother. Tara would be in good hands. All would be well, she chanted.

Jaynie had been scheduled for Sunday as her first day back to work, with Monday off. One day wouldn't be so bad. But, starting next Tuesday, Jaynie would be back to the old grind of a forty-hour work week.

Hang tough for the reward, kiddo.

Her mother's face came to mind. A no-nonsense, stern lady, who'd softened with time. Having given up on men years ago, Elizabeth Winchester had let her hair go steel-gray and had put more than a few extra pounds on her average frame. But she seemed happy now, and for the first time in her life seemed settled in, no longer expectant. She drew her pleasure from good books, quilting and card games with friends she'd made in her middle-management position at a phone company. "This will do," she'd often said to her daughter during their phone conversations. "I don't have any complaints."

Was that all Jaynie had to look forward to? Quilts and card games?

Jaynie knew Tara would be the light of her grandmother's life when she arrived in another week. And the distraction of having a full-time visitor, while working, would help keep her mind off of Terrance.

She walked to the nursery, with Tara tethered to her chest in the sling, to fold some laundry. A strange clanking sound came from her backyard. It sounded like someone was hammering.

"What the…?" Jaynie crossed to the window and pulled back the curtain. She gasped.

There worked Terrance, pounding metal pegs into the ground to stabilize a fully erected tent!

Swishing the curtain closed, she strode to the back door and into her tiny yard.

"Are you crazy?" She strangled the words to keep from yelling.

Terrance swaggered toward her. "Only about you, sweet-cakes." He made a quick right turn and yanked on a rope. The front tent flaps opened, showing Jaynie a small, but efficient area, complete with a bed, sleeping bag, clothes and even a chair.

He'd moved in? Or outside? In a tent? As irritated as she insisted she was feeling, a tiny twinge of amusement skittered through her brain. She covered for it with an indignant pose, one hand cradling Tara, the other planted on her hip.

"Just what do you think you're doing?"

He ambled toward her and took a peek inside the sling. "Hi, Peanut," he said. "I've missed you."

Jaynie swatted his hand away. "Answer my question."

"It seems a certain headstrong, yet beautiful woman doesn't know what's best for her." He stared Jaynie down until her knees went wobbly. "And, since I've finally figured out what's best for *me*, I'll be living here until said woman gets the point."

Her heart jumped to her throat. How could she remain strong with the temptation of Terrance in her very own backyard?

"There is no point to get. You lied to me, took advantage, just so you could be in Tara's life." She clamped her arms around the baby and took several steps back. "You're just a sperm donor. That doesn't make you her real father."

He stared her down. "You and I both know I'm more than that."

Rushing into the house, she slammed the door closed. Tara flinched. Jaynie felt horrible, and quickly soothed her with a pat. Only then did she finish her thoughts. *I wish things could be different.*

She toughened up, looked through the laundry room window, and said, "If you're not out of here in the next hour, I'm calling the police!"

Tara squealed. Terrance folded his arms,

looking resolute. She turned and marched into the kitchen.

Now what do I do?

In Jaynie's backyard, over a small portable hibachi, Terrance barbecued vegetables and a boneless chicken breast. Three hours had passed since he'd set up the tent. He knew she wouldn't call the police. Beneath the rage that filled her eyes, he still saw that look—the look of love.

Taking his sister's advice to heart, he'd come up with this wacky plan. "When it comes to women," she'd said, "persistence pays off."

He vowed to do whatever was necessary. Even if it meant staying camped out in her backyard, however long it took, to get back into her good graces.

Seeing her again just now on the back stoop, he'd felt the passion he had for her slam out of his chest. He needed a moment to recover. God, he missed her—and Tara.

He'd rearranged his entire life to put them at the center, and now he couldn't even get in the back door. But, both patient and resourceful, he'd wait it out, certain it would be only so long before Jaynie couldn't resist him, again.

Dr. Shrinivasan had come through for him. Optimistic joy replaced the gloom he'd been harboring in his heart. For the hell of it, he jumped and swung on a low branch of the tree in her yard—until he smelled smoke and realized his chicken breast had caught fire.

Jaynie systematically went to each window in the house and pulled the shade. She'd shut him out. Block him out of her mind. Whatever it took, she'd do it, to be rid of the man she still loved. She would never be able to trust that he loved her for her and her alone. No. Tara was the reason he'd pledged his heart to her…and that wasn't good enough.

Mrs. Bouchet came and went. Kim and Tommy came for a visit and left. Now Jaynie sat alone in the perfect Feng Shui of her dark living room. She could feel Terrance's life force beckoning, drawing her away from her senses.

She had to resist, stand her ground for what she knew was right. She moved two tall potted plants into the path of his energy force, to block it, and sat down on the couch.

If he didn't truly love her, he'd eventually grow bored and move on, leaving not only Jaynie, but also Tara brokenhearted. She'd never let that happen to her daughter. Not the way it had happened to her, over and over, as a child, with her mother's parade of changing boyfriends.

Jaynie brushed the stubborn ringlets and waves in her hair, preparing for bed. She tried not to think of Terrance, curled up in a sleeping bag, in a tent, in her backyard. Tara slept nearby in the bedside crib. One last check of the apnea monitor and Jaynie was set to climb into bed and attempt to sleep. So many thoughts swirled inside her head that she suspected she'd never be able to fall asleep. But the roiling emotions had drained her, and nursing Tara just minutes before had depleted the last of her physical reserves. Before she knew it, she was fast asleep.

* * *

The first day at work shocked her back into the reality of being a nurse.

Mrs. Bouchet had arrived at the house fifteen minutes early, and they'd gone through a quick checklist. When they'd passed through the kitchen, the sight of Terrance's tent had caught the woman's eye.

Jaynie had covered for the unusual circumstances. "Oh, don't mind him. He's harmless." She'd tried to act casual. "He gets away with practically nothing for rent." She had shaken her head. "Some people," she'd said under her breath as she'd opened the freezer to show Mrs. Bouchet several bags of frozen breast milk.

Jaynie had cried and blubbered as if she was giving her child to an orphanage when it was time to leave. Saying goodbye to Tara was even harder than saying goodbye to Terrance.

But, like remembering how to ride a bicycle, she slipped into the role of charge nurse the minute her crisp uniform and sensible white shoes entered the pulmonary ward and the distinct smell of hospital entered her nostrils.

Several nurses rushed to greet her, as though she were a celebrity. They hugged each other, and Jaynie shared her photographs of Tara with them, sending the ladies into cooing and squealing spells.

Well, she is adorable.

Using good old-fashioned common sense, Jaynie assigned herself to be the medicine nurse. She'd tackle total patient care another day. Today she'd push the gray cart on wheels to every patient's room, and distribute medication as directed by their personal physician's orders.

After end-of-shift report, she delivered everything from antibiotics, to bronchodilators, insulin to IV piggybacks, to the patients on the ward. The routine only allowed time to think about Tara once or twice an hour.

At lunch, after using the breast pump, she called home to check in on how Tara and Mrs. Bouchet were doing.

"Everything is peachy, sweetie. Quit worrying," Mrs. Bouchet said in a friendly tone, just before sneezing. "Tara is a wonderful baby. We've got her right on schedule."

"What do you mean 'we'?" Sudden concern that Mrs. Bouchet had brought a friend over developed in her worrywart head.

"Why, that nice young man who lives in your backyard. Terrance and I. He heard Tara fussing in the kitchen while I was defrosting your breast milk, and he tapped on the door."

Jaynie gasped and bit her tongue. "Ouch."

"What was that dear?" Oblivious, Mrs. Bouchet continued. "He has quite the way with your baby." She sniffed. "Said he always helps out." She blew her nose.

Jaynie worried that the woman might be coming down with a cold, and wanted to snatch Tara away from her germs.

"Oh, and I let him use your shower. I hope you don't mind."

Are you crazy!

Knowing she had to be diplomatic, Jaynie stayed calm. "Mrs. Bouchet, please don't let him into the house again. I should have been more honest this morning. He isn't my friend, and he doesn't really live there. He's my ex-boyfriend and has no business camping in my backyard."

After a suspended silence, Mrs. Bouchet said, "If you say so. But I have thoroughly enjoyed his company—and he's easy on the eyes, too, if you know what I mean." The woman chuckled, and Jaynie imagined her over sixty-five years old chins jiggling.

Going back to work, Jaynie gave out more medicine. She assisted other nurses with treatments for ventilator patients, along with tracheostomy care, and inserted a couple of intravenous lines. She thought about Tara more, and in between worked on staffing schedules for the following month. Before she knew it, it was time to go home.

She drove her car into the driveway of her house, grateful that Terrance wasn't in view. Thank God she had tomorrow off and he would have to work.

Her homecoming with Tara was sublime. The infant's little eyes tried their best to focus on her face. And when Jaynie spoke Tara's tiny tense body relaxed. The obvious recognition of child to mother was a boon to Jaynie's lagging spirit.

Having changed into more comfortable clothes after work, and ready and eager to nurse her baby, she waved goodbye to Mrs. Bouchet and prepared to sit in the rocker.

Thoughts of her and Terrance doing wild and wonderful things in that very seat caused her to change places. She chose the couch, where the pleasant trickling of water over rocks from her indoor fountain could be heard the best. That Feng Shui really had made her house more of a home, she marveled, and fought back the urge to run to the bathroom.

After a long and pleasant nursing session, Tara drifted off to sleep and Jaynie scurried to the shower to refresh herself. She lit a lavender-scented candle, stripped naked and reached inside the shower stall to turn on the water. A note had been taped to the spigot.

Mrs. Bouchet let me use the shower, so I hope you don't mind. I did a lot of thinking about us in here. There's plenty of room to get creative. Look in the back corner. Are you thinking what I'm thinking? Yeah, that would work.

Jaynie splashed water from the faucet onto her face, and groaned.

I got to see our daughter today. I wish I could see you, too. Look, I screwed up. There are things we need to talk about, if you'll just give me a chance.

I miss you, but you know where to find me.

Love, T.

As soon as Jaynie had finished bathing, she closed all the window shades on the back part of the house, and wished there was a reference guide on how to handle a situation like this.

The next morning, up at six for a cup of

herbal tea before Tara woke, Jaynie saw Terrance emerge from the tent. Dressed in jogging shorts and tank top, he caught her watching.

Dang!

Before she could look away, he grinned and waved at her through the window, running down the driveway and onto the street. She lived a good eight miles from Mercy Hospital, but that distance would mean nothing to a health nut like Terrance.

Jaynie imagined all the nurses by the panorama window in the pulmonary ward, waiting for his usual entrance. If they only had a clue what had transpired over the last six weeks, they'd have a gossip feeding frenzy. Thank God Jaynie could trust Kim to keep her mouth shut.

Tuesday started with the same old grind: nurse Tara, greet Mrs. Bouchet, cry and leave for work. The only difference today was that Terrance would be on the job, too. She dreaded the possibility of seeing him there.

Just before seven a.m., Kim came shooting through the double doors. Late again, she waved at Jaynie, whirled around and made a beeline for the nurses' lounge.

Some things never change.

Except Kim looked happier now than Jaynie had ever seen her. Her color was good, she'd put on a few pounds—in the right places—and her eyes glowed with contentment. Jaynie marveled over what love could do for a person, and bitterly remembered how sweet it had been with Terrance for a few weeks. Immediately she put up her guard. Until he left to start medical school it would be a hard, cold fact that he worked at Mercy Hospital, too, and she'd just have to get over it.

At eight o'clock, he rounded the corner to the second floor. Sure enough, he'd assigned himself to the pulmonary ward. Jaynie couldn't stop the spurt of adrenaline. Her heart raced and she grew winded.

He walked right up to her and smiled. "Good morning. How are you feeling?"

How dare you ask how I am?

A flush warmed her cheeks. Steeling herself against his kindness, she answered curtly, "I'm fine," and brushed past him with an intravenous bag in her hand. Quickly she tamped down the urge to treat him like a friend, and strode away.

She could feel his eyes on her back and fought the impulse to turn around.

Don't even think about it.

She'd get past this helpless feeling of love if it was the last thing she ever did.

Jaynie's eyes met with Kim's, which squinted with concern, and then Jaynie noticed several other nurses looking on. Perhaps Kim hadn't been as trustworthy as Jaynie had given her credit for. She glared at Kim, who quickly looked away, guilty as charged—like a child getting caught with her hand in the cookie jar.

Damn. They all know.

Jaynie entered the nearest patient room and pretended she needed to do something of importance. The old gentleman there opened his eyes and watched her bite her lip and squint.

"You look like you could use some cheering up," he said, in a winded voice.

Realizing she wasn't alone, she looked up and smiled at the man in the hospital bed, who battled the last stages of emphysema.

"Oh, it's nothing, Mr. Stein." She walked closer to him. His color was off, and the oxygen saturation interpreter clipped on his finger registered below eighty-nine percent, setting off the monitor. The loud beeping reminded her of Tara's apnea device, but in this case it wasn't a false alarm.

Mr. Stein grew more short of breath. He struggled to inhale, his bony shoulders lifting with each attempt. Jaynie's first response was to increase his oxygen, but she knew with emphysema patients it would only trap more air in his lungs, preventing him from taking in a deep breath, so she left it at one liter.

After readjusting the pulse oximeter on his finger, to make sure it wasn't reflective of cold hands and poor circulation, the saturation dropped even more. She moved the bedside table over his hospital bed and helped him sit up and forward, placing his arms across two pillows on the table. Knowing the position would help open his lung expansion and hopefully allow some air inside, she waited for results.

"Do some pursed-lip breathing, Mr. Stein," she suggested, and puckered her own mouth while he slowly exhaled against the pressure of his lips. If he could get some of the trapped air out, he'd be able to take in more oxygenated air.

The saturation reading dropped to eighty-seven.

His lips were faintly discolored, the fine capillaries on his face looked blue, and his eyes tensed with concern.

One last attempt to readjust his pulse oximeter proved fruitless. The loud beeping continued as Mr. Stein's oxygen declined.

Answering the equipment alarm, Terrance brushed into the room, greeted the patient, quickly assessed the saturation levels, and fished some vials out from his lab jacket. After setting up a handheld nebulizer for Mr. Stein, he kept busy.

Jaynie watched while Terrance worked, calmly and efficiently, like the expert he was. He did have a gift and he should pursue medicine, even if it meant moving to another state.

His long, lean runner's body moved with an ease and purpose that she admired against her will.

While holding Mr. Stein's hand for moral support, she read the patient chart and realized he was a DNR—do not resuscitate—and had requested never to be put on a ventilator.

Unconsciously, she grasped his hand a little tighter. The old gentleman nodded his head appreciatively as a silent understanding passed between them.

"After the breathing treatment, I'll do some postural drainage," Terrance said. "We'll get that stubborn mucus out of your lungs."

The patient looked grateful. Jaynie could see his skinny shoulders relax while Terrance auscultated his lungs and then checked his pulse. He looked at Jaynie and nodded, assuring her all would be well. Only then did her nerves unwind.

She left the room and stood outside, considering how dreadful it must be for Mr. Stein to know that one day he would slowly suffocate from his disease…and die.

After a long percussion session, and a symphony of coughing and throat clearing sounds, Terrance emerged from Mr. Stein's room victorious. He sought out Jaynie with intense hazel eyes.

"Well, he's back up to ninety percent oxygen saturation, and feeling a heck of a lot better." Terrance raised a clear specimen jar of discolored sputum. "I think he may have developed an infection. I'll run this to the lab for some cultures."

Quickly averting her eyes—sputum had never been something Jaynie could tolerate looking at—she pretended to have an unnatural interest in the syringe she held. She flashed a glance at Terrance and said, "Thanks for your help." Curt. To the point. Then she moved away, so as not to encourage any further conversation.

Morbid thoughts seemed to color the rest of her day on the ward filled with respiratorially challenged patients. The only bright spot was thinking about her daughter, and how she longed to go home to hold her in her arms.

At the end of the day, though tired, she walked briskly to her car in the employee lot, eager to get home. Opening the door, she heard someone running up behind her.

"Jaynie, wait."

It was Terrance.

She refused to turn around, just stood there shaking her head. When he came up behind her, she spoke. "Please leave me alone. I can't deal with this."

He whispered over her shoulder. "I'm not going away. I just want you to know that."

She felt his breath warm her neck and reacted against her will. She'd changed her clothes in the nurses' lounge, and pulled her hair up into a ponytail, and now she felt chills run down her spine.

Damn him.

He sped off in his jogging shorts and running shoes, as quickly as he'd come, leaving her more confused than ever. Why make a promise he knew he could never keep—*I'm not going away*—when his plans were to quit working at the hospital and attend out-of-state medical school? Why torment her with hope? She ran her hand across her neck and got into the car, turning the ignition.

All men went away. Ask her mother. She'd tell the truth. Jaynie remembered everything just like it was yesterday. The men would wander into Mom's life, make themselves at home, and then, just when she and her mother had gotten used to them, pack up and leave. And when Jaynie had given her long-term boy-friend the ultimatum to marry or move…he'd left, too.

She shook her head, quickly becoming distracted at the sight of Terrance in his skimpy running trunks sprinting down the road as she passed in the car. For all she knew, considering traffic lights, he'd probably beat her home.

Ten minutes later, when she parked the car and found Papa Gino, Terrance's cat, on her doorstep, she about screamed.

No! You may not weasel yourself into my life, Terrance.

The first thing she did, after greeting her baby with a big kiss, and before Terrance arrived in her backyard, was once again close all of the window shades.

What I don't see can't hurt me.

Feeling content that she was standing her ground, she went about her evening routine, trying with all her might to pretend that the man she loved wasn't camped out in her backyard.

A loud blaring sound drove her from the pleasant dream she was having about a handsome man with strong arms carrying her away to paradise.

Loud. Blaring.

Jaynie awoke to the dreadful apnea monitor alarm. Half asleep, she wondered which lead had come undone this time. She stared at her daughter, completely still, who'd somehow managed to squirm into the corner of her bed. She switched on the bedside light and saw that all three leads were in place.

"Tara?" She gently massaged the baby to stimulate her breathing, but there was no response. "Tara!" she called again, gently tapping and shaking the sole of her foot, but still no response.

She'd stopped breathing.

Jaynie's hand shot to her mouth. "Oh, my God! Tara!"

As she lifted the infant from the crib and laid her across the bed, she screamed for Terrance. He was at her side in an instant, dressed in his underwear.

"Tara's not breathing," she said. "Call 911!"

Looking wild-eyed, he dashed for the phone. Jaynie gently tilted back Tara's head.

"Breathe, Tara, breathe!" She checked the baby's airway, lifted her chin with one fingertip and looked, listened and felt for breath.

How could this be happening? Her baby had been thriving more each day, gaining weight, blossoming. Jaynie had to fight off the panicking mother to reach the seasoned nurse within.

Do infant rescue breathing. Quick!

Keeping Tara's head back and chin lifted, Jaynie placed her mouth over the baby's nose and mouth, then carefully gave two puffs. Her little chest lifted and fell; nothing blocked her airway. Yet the infant didn't breathe on her own. She checked her brachial pulse. Thank God, her heart was still beating.

"Yes, I have an emergency," she heard Terrance say. "Our baby has stopped breathing."

Fear surged through every fiber of her body, but Jaynie fought it. She breathed for her baby every three seconds. "Come on, Tara, breathe."

The area around the baby's face was starting to turn faintly blue. So were her fingertips. Jaynie breathed for her again. And again.

Oh, my God!

In a trance, she felt her heart palpitating as she felt for her baby's brachial pulse. Nothing. Horror filled her mind.

And from the corner of her eye Jaynie saw Terrance drop the phone as she started cardio-pulmonary resuscitation.

Tara's heart had stopped.

CHAPTER TEN

Two emergency medical technicians barreled into the house with the finesse of a herd of elephants. And, with them, the world as Jaynie knew it came crashing down at her feet. They stormed the kitchen, carrying armloads of equipment, adding to the chaos in her mind.

Shouting back and forth between Terrance, Jaynie and themselves, they said, "SIDS. Rebreathing asphyxia. Blunted response. Hypoxemia. Hypercarbia."

Jaynie moved out of their way. She stood on her toes and shifted her weight from one foot to the other, determined to keep her daughter in sight while they worked.

Terrance identified himself as a respiratory

therapist and asked for an airway. His voice sounded distant.

"What's the smallest you've got in your kit?" His eyes never wavered from Tara's still form.

"2.5 millimeter," the larger man dressed in navy blue said, while rifling through a red three-tiered box. He handed a tiny white plastic question-mark-shaped item to Terrance.

The other man held a penlight above Tara's mouth, shining it toward the back of her throat.

With the skill of an expert, Terrance slipped the airway device inside Tara's mouth and carefully down her throat. Jaynie knew this was insurance against an obstructed respiratory passage. In mere seconds his mission was accomplished, and the other rescue worker had connected oxygen and an infant Ambu-Bag to act like a bellows for her lungs.

Until she could breathe for herself, they'd breathe for her. Jaynie shuddered. She wouldn't allow herself to think anything negative. Things would be okay. She paced and prayed.

"All clear?" one man said, holding little paddles against Tara's chest.

They gave a quick electrical shock, waited and watched for a spontaneous rhythm on the monitor. When nothing happened they continued with external compressions, and a few seconds later shocked her again.

Minutes that seemed like hours later, one of the emergency techs made an announcement.

"Sinus rhythm." He'd discovered a faint heartbeat, and indicated the blip on the defibrillation machine.

Thinking the rhythmical beep of the machine was the most beautiful thing she'd ever heard, Jaynie exchanged a relieved look with Terrance, and finally took a breath.

Tara would live.

Hours later at the hospital, when Jaynie's trembling hands had steadied, and Dr. Shrinivasan had reassured her for the third time that all would be well, she relaxed the tiniest bit.

"It appears that Tara has a respiratory virus that may have shut down her airways."

A quick flash to Mrs. Bouchet with her sniffles and sneezes over the last week came to Jaynie's mind. A virus had caused this? Guilt bit like a rabid dog.

Why didn't I stay home with her?

"Due to the baby's premature lungs, the lack of oxygen did not trigger the response that we would normally observe," he said.

Dizzy with anxiety, she couldn't stop thinking over what might have been if she hadn't had the apnea monitor in place. Jaynie needed to sit down. She searched for a chair...anything.

She'd been aware of her constant companion over the last few hours, taken him for granted, even. But not until the moment she lost her balance and Terrance caught her in his arms did she quietly thank God he'd been there throughout the ordeal.

"Thank you," she whispered, leaning on him.

He held her steady and firm against his

chest. She felt him take a breath of relief along with hers.

Feeling as if she owed everyone an explanation, she began to talk. "I had a little wedge under her back so she could sleep on her side. Somehow she'd rolled onto her stomach." Jaynie bit back tears and overcame panic while she replayed the moment in her head. "I found her...in the corner of the bed."

From behind, Terrance grasped her arms and gave a firm squeeze of support.

"Thank God for the apnea monitor," she said.

"You did everything right," Dr. Shrinivasan said with a mild nod and a reassuring smile. "These things happen. And thanks be to God for your neighbor, no?"

A smile broke across her lips. "Yes." *My hero.* She turned to Terrance and hugged him. With the ease of lifetime friends, he wrapped her in his arms and kissed the top of her head. His chest vibrated beneath her cheek.

A millisecond before she'd snuggled in close she'd glimpsed a troubled squint in his eyes, a tension that tightened his lips. For a man who preferred action to feelings, he seemed frazzled and worn out with emotion. She massaged the tense muscles in his back and refrained from saying a word. They stood and gently rocked back and forth in their comforting embrace for what seemed like eternity, until their breathing became synchronized.

With Tara safely resuscitated, and sleeping quietly under an oxy-hood for a night of hospital observation, Jaynie and Terrance made their way to the parents' lounge to sit. They held hands, but didn't say a word.

Somewhere along the way Terrance's hand dropped free and his mood shifted. She felt his palm tremble as he guided her at the small of her back. She glanced at him. His skin had gone pale. A distant gaze had settled into his eyes, and he seemed to be grappling with the magnitude of what had happened.

She'd read studies about people who performed flawlessly under fire, but once everything was over they fell apart. Maybe he was one of those people. No. That didn't seem like Terrance. At least, she hoped not.

After minutes of silence, while he stared intensely into nothingness, he scrubbed his face and shook his head. As though he'd come to some sort of conclusion, he turned and watched Jaynie with sad eyes, earnestly searching every inch of her face. For what? Understanding? Forgiveness? Her gut tightened with a bad premonition.

He stood. In anticipation, she did, too. Terrance backed away, held up his hands in surrender, pleading with his eyes until a bleak hazel glare of defeat overcame his expression. He shook his head again and said, "I can't do this. I thought I could, but I can't. It's too much. I'm sorry."

He walked off, leaving her, stunned and breathless, to collapse into the nearest chair. Alone.

Two days later Tara was back home and in perfect form, demanding all of her mother's attention. Thankful for the distraction, Jaynie showered her with love.

Myriad questions circled in her head, but the same answer repeated itself. A sad realization crept up like a stealthy shadow in the night. Terrance couldn't take the demands of fatherhood…so he'd bowed out of their lives.

Granted, she hadn't made it easy for him—refusing to let him in, punishing him for being honest with her. But when it had come down to the line, when they'd almost lost Tara, he hadn't been able to take it. He'd packed up his tent and left her yard…and their lives.

This was the way it was supposed to be from the beginning, she kept reminding herself.

I wanted to be a single parent. I wanted Tara all to myself.

Another overused saying from her mother popped into her head. "Be careful what you wish for…it may come true."

With Tara in the sling, Jaynie snuggled against her head and glanced at the pile of books on single parenting on the floor. She'd checked them out from the library. On top was the title *A Happy Mother Makes a Happy Baby*.

I'll have to work on that.

Noticing Tara had drifted off to sleep in the sling, and since there was no time like the present, she walked across the perfect Feng Shui of her living room, picked up a book to read and sat in the infamous rocking chair. She planned to move on with her life, but today she needed a reminder that she hadn't always been alone. She vowed to remember and savor her days and hours with Terrance. They hadn't been nearly long enough, but if it was all she'd have, she'd make them stretch across her lifetime.

A quiet tapping on her front door drew her attention. She opened it to a glorious bright day and an angelic silhouette. Sun-glare danced off the most beautiful natural shade of red hair Jaynie had ever seen. Miles of it.

A warm breeze scented with apple blossom blew across her face, and a petite pregnant woman smiled at Jaynie.

"Hello. I'm Tara—Terrance's sister. May I come in?"

Jaynie went loose in recognition. She swept the door wide and invited her in with a gesture, unable to find her voice.

"I've been told I have a niece." Her eyes glanced to the sling and the child within. "I couldn't stay away."

So similar to Terrance in mannerisms, yet her facial features—beyond an identical smile—would never give their relationship away. Where he was robust, she was elf-like. He was broad and strong, she was delicate and narrow—except for where her pregnancy protruded. Yet Jaynie saw traces of the same little girl who had won her over in the childhood picture from the cryobank. A special spirit lived in her eyes, and the reason she named her daughter Tara couldn't be denied. Immediately, Jaynie liked her.

They sat across from each other in silence, until Jaynie offered her most precious gift. "Would you like to hold her?" Removing the straps of the snuggling sling, Jaynie released her daughter and watched the older Tara's eyes light up.

Oh, there it was again. The self-same smile. Terrance was indeed her twin brother.

Two cups of herbal tea later, and an abundance of superficial dialogue followed by a diaper change, Tara Jr. drifted off to sleep again. Jaynie felt as if she'd made a new friend over the last hour, and she sensed that the feeling was mutual.

Aunt Tara reached inside her purse and fished out an old and tattered picture. "I thought you'd like to have the original. Terry told me about how Peanut got her name." Her hazel-green eyes and her smile brightened an already gleaming face. "I can't tell you how honored I am."

"I never intended to find out who the father was," Jaynie said, and reached for the photo to study it. "I'm afraid I turned your brother's life upside down. I never meant to."

"The idiot needed it." She raised an eyebrow and crossed her arms with the spunk of a sister.

"He wanted to be Peter Pan all his life. It was about time someone or something kicked his butt into growing up."

"But I don't want Tara to dash his dreams. It was all my doing."

"He wanted to come here today, to invite you and Peanut for dinner at his house tonight. But I suggested I come instead. I thought maybe he'd been pushing you too hard, and you might need some space. And I wanted to give you the picture myself." Tara rose and opened her arms for a hug. "I hope you'll go. He needs you. You have no idea."

Her words sounded heaven-sent.

He needs me.

Jaynie followed Tara's lead and they embraced. Dainty, like a thin teenager, she smelled like plumeria bath gel. And Jaynie felt like she'd found a long-lost friend.

"Regardless of what happens," Tara said, reaching for Jaynie's hands, "I'd like to keep in touch."

"I'd like that," she said, squeezing back.

Hesitant to accept the invitation for dinner, but longing to see Terrance again, Jaynie considered the significance of the request. Maybe they needed an official goodbye.

"What time?"

Papa Gino looked bored where he sat on the porch of Terrance's house, like a large gray furry pear. He suspiciously watched Jaynie approach, and when she'd reached the halfway point scurried off to the nearby bushes in a blur. Terrance busted out the door with a heartbreaking smile.

"Hey, let me get that," he said, rushing to her side to fetch the diaper bag and baby seat. "Anything else you need?" He glanced toward the car.

He'd tied his hair back, and wore a pressed button-down mint-green shirt rolled up at the cuffs with dark pants. Jaynie felt somewhat underdressed in casual post-pregnancy elastic waistband pants and a plain pullover top.

Drawing close, his strong hand retrieved the

bag. She caught a musky forest cologne scent and memorized it, wondering if after today she'd ever have the opportunity again. It was obvious that he'd gone all out for her, and it touched her heart.

He smiled again, a long, sexy, confident smile, as if she was the only woman he'd ever seen. Flutters started in her chest and fanned across her stomach. Her eyes widened, and she needed to adjust her glasses on her nose. Her lips pinched into a tense response, and she tightened her grasp around Tara for support. He wouldn't stop looking at her, which made her feel uncomfortable, so she cleared her throat.

"Shall we go inside?" She pushed the point.

"Oh, sure." After peeking at Tara in the baby sling, goo-gooing a syllable or two, and more grinning, he led the way to the house.

Compared to the rustic wood exterior, the interior of his home was uncluttered and inviting. A large dark leather armchair sat across from a soft brown couch and a heavy wood coffee table. A redbrick fireplace covered three-quarters of an entire wall. A sliding glass door overlooked a verdant backyard forest of overgrown bushes, trees and shrubs. The room hadn't changed since she'd last been here. It smelled freshly aired out by the breeze, but a hint of last night's fireplace smoke lingered.

Terrance hurried to put the bag and baby seat down, and then reached for Tara. "May I?"

Jaynie handed him the baby, and he received her as if she was the most precious gift on earth. He held her close to his chest, took a deep whiff of her baby smell and kissed the top of her head. A pained look of loss filled his eyes as he studied his daughter.

"She's so beautiful." A soft fatherly smile crossed his lips. He lifted thick brown lashes to look at Jaynie. "We did good, huh?"

"The best."

"Astounding," he said.

They stood in tortured silence for several seconds while Jaynie contemplated their circumstances. He'd obviously invited her over for a reason, and she thought she knew why she'd come, but neither was ready to get to the point. She really didn't want to find out that, as she'd always imagined, she'd spend the rest of her life alone.

Seeming a tiny bit nervous, Terrance said, "Listen, I've got a few more things to do before dinner is ready. Why don't you sit down and make yourself comfortable? I'll bring you some watered-down wine and put on some music."

"Should I be drinking?"

"I've read that a little wine helps the milk let down," he said, and grinned. "But you've never had a problem with that, have you?"

He winked, bringing back memories of those few embarrassing moments with Terrance when she'd unexpectedly leaked. The beginnings of a blush started at her neck. She could feel heat rise up her cheeks.

Still grinning, and now within reach, he tugged on the sling left around her neck. "May I borrow this?"

Shaken by his intimate gesture, Jaynie removed the pale pink cloth and handed it to him. His warm, strong grasp held hers longer than necessary. She didn't want to let go, either. She avoided his eyes while helping him put on the baby sling. She tried not to react to the closeness while adjusting the length, and quickly slid Tara inside. Standing back and assessing her handiwork, she saw him set off for the kitchen. It touched her more than she dared allow.

Jaynie took a deep breath and relaxed into the couch. After removing her shoes, she put her feet up on the heavy dark wood table. She enjoyed being in Terrance's space, soaking up the essence of him with every detail.

A pair of antique tennis rackets hung crisscrossed on one wall; a picture of a humongous wave with a minuscule surfer emerging from the curl hung on another. An old-fashioned toboggan held wood logs for the fireplace. An authentic fire hydrant stand held a huge bowl of spicy scented pinecones.

She'd always thought the house suited him. Would he find a home where he belonged out of state?

Forced out of her thoughts by an ice-cold glass being placed in her hand, she startled, almost slopping the drink over the rim. Composing herself, she thanked him. He plopped down next to her on the couch, baby in tow.

"Everything's set. When the timer goes off, dinner will be ready." He removed Tara from the sling and held her above him with extended arms while guarding her fragile neck. Her legs kicked with freedom, and Terrance and Jaynie grinned at each other.

"Look at those perfect little feet," he said.

Bit by bit Jaynie relaxed, and before dinner was served, against her will, she'd reaffirmed her love for him. Life had really punched a cruel wallop this time around. By accident, she'd found the man she could love for a lifetime but would never have. And, because of her, he'd become a father—something he'd never wanted to be except as an anonymous donor.

As if he'd read her thoughts, he placed Tara in the crook of his arm and reached for Jaynie's hand with the other. He brought it to his mouth and kissed each fingertip, sending a regiment of goosebumps marching up her arm. His hazel-golden eyes carefully watched her face. She blinked, and tried desperately not to give herself away.

"After dinner, we need to talk," he whispered.

Afraid to appear too eager, she stopped herself from nodding a millisecond before the timer went off.

Pasta, bread, salad—a bachelor's wonder meal—tasted better to Jaynie than she could ever remember. And if her stomach hadn't been tied up in a knot she would have eaten more. He said the special tang of the sauce had something to do with balsamic vinegar. Feeling gullible, she bought his culinary boast, never once suspecting the sauce might have come out of a jar until she saw an empty one sitting on the counter.

She glanced into her pasta bowl. Well, at least the mushrooms looked fresh.

Filling her tummy with such delectable food, and her mind with naughty thoughts, he'd done a good job of convincing her that packaged tomato sauce was a gourmet delight.

He obviously enjoyed watching her eat, but behind his encouraging stare she could see traces of the same hesitation she'd seen at the hospital. Hints of sleepless shadows circled his eyes. She could tell he was as wrung out as she over their situation. What the heck was the next step?

Once again on the same wavelength, he opened up.

"When I was camping in your yard, I had made up my mind. I was certain I wanted to be with you and Tara."

Jaynie stopped mid-chew, thinking she'd heard wrong.

He hesitated. "Then, after we almost lost Tara the other night, I knew my original decision to never have kids again was the right one." Terrance stopped eating, held a piece of bread in his hand and tore it apart—along with Jaynie's heart. "I just can't handle the thought of losing someone I love again." Unable to make eye contact, he said, "I'm sorry."

The watered-down wine had acted like a truth serum on Jaynie. With a quick burst of anger, she fought back. "So it's safer to never love or get attached rather than experience loss? What kind of chicken-hearted quality of life is that?"

He nodded, and sniffed with agreement.

"You risk your own life every time you go rock-climbing, and you don't seem to care how it will affect your parents, or your sister—the people that love you the most. Oh, but if someone *you* love stumbles and falls, that's not fair?" She raised her palms. "No offense, Terrance, but you sound like a coward."

He popped the wad of bread into his mouth and chewed ruggedly. "Yeah, well, if the shoe fits..." Stirring uncomfortably in his chair, he reached for the Parmesan cheese. "I guess I'll have to wear it."

Jaynie thought about biting her tongue. But why not lay it all on the table? She might never have the chance again, and what did she have to lose? And what did he mean when he kept saying "again"? As if this wasn't the first time he'd almost lost someone.

"You're better than that, Terrance. I know it."

He squinted, still not making eye contact, and pinched his lips before speaking. "You deserve better than me. That much I know."

A wry laugh escaped her lips. "What a noble cop-out."

He sat straighter, finally looking at her, carefully considering her comment.

"There's something else you need to know."

Oh, God. What other bombshell could he drop? That'd he'd met and befriended another one of his sperm beneficiaries?

"I had a daughter named Emily once. Being Tara's mom, you must know how much love I felt. I didn't really want to be a dad at twenty-three, but I was willing to accept responsibility." Water formed in his eyes. "She was incredible." His lips quivered and he tensed them. Once he regained his composure, he continued. "I loved her like nothing else in my life before." Tears brimmed. "And then, one day, she didn't wake up." He fought back the tears, but they fell anyway. "I wasn't a dad anymore. Just like that." He used the cuff of his hand to swipe away his sadness.

Jaynie wept silently.

"I didn't know how to save Emily. And when Tara was slipping through my fingers and I couldn't do anything about it..." Terrance stopped to catch his breath. He continued in a controlled voice. "It was like the same nightmare again. I couldn't bear to go through it. What kind of father is that?"

Silence engulfed the room like a confessional booth. Jaynie's heart wrenched with empathy for Terrance. Of course he'd never want to go through such sadness again.

"I had no idea. I'm so sorry, Terrance." They grasped hands and clung tightly to each other.

But Tara was alive, dammit. And she deserved a relationship with her biological father.

She swallowed hard and steadied her voice.

"I discovered something in all the reading I've done this past week," she said. "My baby needs a happy mother, and I'm not sure how happy I can be alone…now that I've found you." She reached for his hand. He didn't pull away.

"You opened a new world for me, too, Jaynie. You and Tara." He squeezed against her firm grasp.

Fighting the desire to turn and run out the door, Jaynie shut her eyes and forced herself to continue. If she couldn't have the ending she dreamed about for herself, at least she could be an advocate for what was best for her daughter. On a deep breath, she spoke her mind.

"You're a man who likes to take risks. Well, I'd like to challenge you to the biggest adventure of your life. Be a father to your daughter."

A pained look crossed his eyes. She didn't give him a chance to respond.

"You don't have to love me, or come around to see me, but for gosh sakes, be a father to Tara. All I'm asking is for you to check in with her on the important dates: her birthday, Father's

Day, Christmas, a couple of weeks in the summer. Is that too much to ask? You're a wonderful person, and now that you've been outed as her dad, she deserves to know you. I promise not to get in your way."

"You'd never be in my way, Jaynie." He took her hand and pressed it to his mouth. "And you didn't let me finish my thought."

A ragged inhalation didn't deliver enough oxygen to her brain. She hadn't fathomed how hard it would be to speak her mind, and, feeling woozy, she squeezed his hand for support.

Clearing his throat, he said, "The thing is, after fighting with myself for the last few days, I don't have any intention of leaving you. I can't. I love you too much."

What had he just said? A shot of adrenaline cleared her head. After a double take, she settled in to his sincere hazel stare. From the look in those eyes, he meant what he'd just said. Her heart skittered around her chest while she hyperventilated and tried to focus, realizing what he'd admitted and knowing it was for real.

"My sister—" he smirked "—in a not so subtle way, kicked my butt into rethinking my original decision. And Dr. Shrinivasan went to the wall for me."

He kissed her fingers until she thought he'd eat her hands. Jaynie wanted to giggle, but was too breathless to utter a sound.

"I've worked it all out. I've been offered a free ride at Mercy Hospital University for med school. I won't have to sell my house *or* leave the state. I'll work a couple days a week to keep up my medical insurance for you and Tara." A handsome smile stretched across his strong jaw and his eyes sparkled with delight. "And, if you don't want to work full time, you can stay home with our daughter a few more days a week."

Simultaneously, a giddy snicker of relief crossed their lips.

"That is, if you'll consider my offer…"

At that, Jaynie gasped. He intercepted her hand before it could reach her mouth, and covered it with extra kisses.

"I've never been more scared about anything in my life," he said. "But this rush of feelings I have about you and Tara is more exciting than skydiving, bungee-jumping and hang-gliding all put together. Now that I know what love is, I want to roll with it."

Shaking her head in disbelief at the turn of events, she felt her chin quiver. She refused to let her feelings fog the opportunity of the moment. It was too important.

"But you only came to me because of Tara. If you hadn't thought she was your daughter you'd never have given me a second chance." Holding on to his hands like an anchor in the storm, she clutched as best as she could, and smiled. "I'm no fool, Terrance."

"I could never love a fool." His penetrating eyes paralyzed her resistance. "It's you that excites me."

"More than white-water rapids?" she asked.

"More than snowboarding the Alps," he said. "You've got *it*, and I want it all with you."

For long, wondrous moments they gazed at

each other in silence. Jaynie's joyous heartbeat pulsed in her head.

"The thing is," Terrance said, "I want Tara to have a happy mom, too. You've got to understand that, long before Tara, I had a big thing for you, Nurse Winchester. The way you strutted around that pulmonary ward with your fine figure and fancy uniforms about drove me crazy."

Her cheeks grew hot and her eyes wide. This was what she'd longed—no, *needed*—to hear. "You did?"

He removed her glasses in a quick, yet delicate manner. "You can't imagine how often I've fantasized about your big brown eyes and sexy mouth." He traced the outline of her lips with a hot finger. "Remembering how it felt to kiss you." His smile was wicked and playful. He traced her jaw upward, toward her ear.

Unable to resist, she leaned into his palm. "I had a few fantasies about you, too."

"Before we ever dated, I used to schedule myself to work on your ward just so I could be near you," he said. "I always wondered what it would be like to help you let your hair down." His fingers weaved through her tight curls. "Man, even with my exceptional imagination, I had no idea how terrific it could really be."

"Really?"

"Oh, yeah, *really*."

Her heart fluttered out of control in her chest and his face grew blurry. She blinked to focus back in, and tried to swallow.

He bit his lower lip and then cleared his throat—again. "You've got to believe me when I tell you that I wanted you long before you ever got pregnant. I kicked myself from one end of the hospital to the other after we broke up. And I was on the verge of asking you out again when you first started showing and the word around the hospital came that you were pregnant. I figured you'd moved on—found someone else."

"You're kidding, right?"

"Ask Dave how bummed out I was about that. He'll back me up." He shook his head. "But what a great stroke of luck. You chose me from the list of all the other donors. Doesn't that prove we were meant to be together?"

"It proves I had great taste when it came to picking genes."

"You chose me," he whispered. "I believe it was meant to be."

A rush of emotion whirled in her head—he did have a good point. Something about his profile had called out to her from the start. And when she'd read his essay and seen that childhood picture, there hadn't been a thread of doubt about who to choose. Her ears rang with excitement. Feeling suspended in time, Jaynie practically levitated on her chair. "You may be on to something."

Terrance squirmed a little in his seat and looked into his lap. "What I'm trying to ask is..." His gaze lifted to her eyes. Sincerity delved into her soul. "Will you marry me?"

Relief and joy burst over the moment, sending all doubt into hiding. Love and hope replaced the fear that had had a stronghold on her heart only seconds before.

Without feeling her usual need to do research, or read two books on the subject of predestination and marriage first, she simply knew in her gut what to say. She beamed at Terrance—the man of her dreams—reeling with joy.

Finally finding her voice, Jaynie answered, "Oh, yes. Tara and I will marry you."

They grinned like the fools in love they were, and laughed at the wondrous change of events. Her single-minded plan for motherhood had backfired. This was the day of all days for Jaynie, and she could never have predicted it.

She rode a swell of joy as if she was on a magic carpet ride, and at her side sat the man she loved with all of her heart and soul.

Unsure of how they'd got there, Jaynie and Terrance stood together, shaking, embracing and consoling each other with hugs. He took her face into his warm hands and gave her a special kiss of promise. She inhaled the earthy scent of the man she loved and relished the moment with a soft, moist vow of her own.

Tightening her knees for support, she returned his kiss with every ounce of love stirring in her heart. And long, luscious moments later, when the kiss that pledged a lifetime together came to an end, they exploded with laughter and joy.

Suddenly remembering Tara across the room in her baby seat, still and quiet, as if she knew something special was going on, Terrance flew to her side and swept her into his arms. He kissed her pudgy pink cheeks and brought the baby, like a gift, to Jaynie.

Again, they grinned at each other in delight, and cooed over the child they had made together as strangers. Long before they'd completely discovered each other and fallen in love they had created Tara with their genes. Now, sustained by love, the anonymous experiment of nine months before had become the chance of a lifetime for true happiness.

And, together, Jaynie, Terrance and Tara would finally be the family they were meant to be.

They looked on with wonder as Tara

squirmed and fussed in Terrance's arms. She twisted up her face and turned pink with effort and concentration, following up with a larger sound than either of them could ever have imagined. And when she had finished her display, Jaynie quickly realized something.

It was time for a diaper change.

EPILOGUE

Ten months later...

CHAOS couldn't begin to describe what was going on at the Zanderson residence. Friends and relatives milled around the overpacked rooms, bumping shoulders and elbows, mumbling pardons and trying not to spill their celebration punch. Jaynie grinned at the sight. The smell of strawberry icing permeated the room. And at the center, in her highchair, sat Princess Tara, wearing a lopsided pink cone hat held in place by with a thin elastic strap under her chin. The sight clutched at Jaynie's heart.

Tara dutifully held up one finger whenever anyone asked, "How old are you today?" And topped off her talent with a sticky four-tooth grin.

She'd never had another episode of apnea after that one close call ten months earlier. She'd grown healthy and robust, and was blossoming into a beautiful little girl, and Jaynie thanked God for that. She was petite for a one-year-old, and her shiny coral party dress seemed to swallow her up, but Tara didn't mind at all. Loving being the center of everyone's attention, she kicked her white patent leather Mary-Jane-clad feet and squealed with delight when Daddy brought the birthday cake toward her. A huge candle sat at the center, surrounded by sugar bunnies and puppies chasing each other's tails around the number one.

"Da-Da. Kay?" Her hazel-green eyes sparkled and her plump hands shot to her hair, comprised of wispy honey-red ringlets.

Though only early April, the California sun glowed bright. Terrance wore a loud Hawaiian shirt with khaki shorts and sandals, and a grin broader than the international happy-face sign. "It's your birthday cake, Peanut. How old are you today?"

Out popped Tara's index finger, accompanied by yet another joyful peep. Her eyes widened and she palmed her cheeks, holding her mouth in an "oh" when everyone in the room began to sing the birthday song.

Through blurry eyes Jaynie watched her daughter beam and squirm with excitement. Joy, thick as the icing on the cake, filled her veins and burst into her heart. Her voice quavered through the anthem along with everyone else's. Her mother stepped beside her and put her arm around her waist. They exchanged the special look only mothers understand.

Kim, decked out in red satin pedal-pushers and an off-the-shoulder top, snapped several pictures, while Tommy, her newly betrothed, ran the digital movie camera. It was hard to tell what gleamed more—the camera flash, or Kim's huge engagement diamond.

Aunt Tara stood across the room with her six-month-old baby glued to her hip and her strapping husband by her side. Fidgeting, and eager to get in on the action, their son reached with both arms and screeched in protest when his mother held him tight in place. The picture of health and single-mindedness, the baby resisted his mother's firm grasp.

The scene evoked so much emotion that the rush of blood made Jaynie feel lightheaded. She searched out and sat down in the nearest chair before the song ended.

"Yay!" Everyone cheered at the end, and Tara clapped her hands.

"Mo," she said, demanding more singing.

Such a simple request couldn't be denied. Terrance started the refrain again, and everyone else joined in. His eyes roamed the room until they found Jaynie. The grin on his face faded the tiniest bit when he saw her.

"Are you okay?" he mouthed, from across the room.

She nodded, clapped her hands and smiled back at him, pretending to sing at the top of her lungs.

Peanut was a daddy's girl. The sun and the

moon rose and set with his presence. And the adoration was mutual. Even though he worked tirelessly in medical school, he allowed for abundant time with his daughter. Jaynie loved their interaction, and only felt jealous of their special bond once in a while.

But not today.

Today she was glad to let Terrance run the show. She'd been feeling weak and nauseated all morning—heck, all week—and the smell of fresh frosting almost made her hurl earlier, when she'd been decorating the cake.

Her mother returned from the kitchen and handed Jaynie a glass of water, with a raised eyebrow and a worried look pasted on her face.

"Thanks," Jaynie said. "I'm okay." She was doing a poor job of convincing her mother everything was fine. But what a rotten time to come down with the flu—and it wasn't even the right season.

An hour later, after every conceivable toddler gift had been torn open and put on display, the cake had been served and the leftover ice cream had melted on the paper plates, Terrance made his way over to his wife. Most of the guests had left. Aunt Tara entertained both babies on the living room floor.

"What's up? You look exhausted." His face betrayed his worry.

"I'm just a little tired. Do I look that bad?" Her hand went to her cheek, then ran self-consciously through some ringlets and hooked them behind her ear.

He shook his head. "You never look bad to me. Maybe just a little pale?" He knelt down next to her and released the very curls she'd just pulled back.

She rested her head on his sturdy shoulder and sighed. "This was great."

"The best," he said, his hand cupping her neck.

Now was as good a time as any, she decided.

"We've been so busy, with work and school and planning everything, that I haven't had a chance to talk to you."

He kissed her cheek. "I know. I've missed you. Are you sure you're okay?"

His warm hazel gaze studied her with both a look of love and of concern pinching at the corner of his eyes.

"Well, actually, I think I may need to take a test."

He hoisted a brow. "What kind of test?"

"Maybe a blood test. Maybe I'm just anemic. I don't know. But I wanted to ask you something first."

"Shoot." He looked eager to get to the heart of her story, and held her hand with a tight, encouraging grasp.

"After you donated to the sperm bank, you said you made sure that you'd never have kids again?"

He straightened his spine and she saw a light-bulb go off in his eyes. He cleared his throat. "Yeah, I signed up for a vasectomy." Now he was looking sheepish, and his eyes betrayed his change of heart. "But I never actually went through with it, though."

After wanting to crown him for never bothering to tell her that part of the story, Jaynie felt

relief wash over her and brighten her mood
from night to day.

"So maybe there isn't anything wrong with me
that a simple home pregnancy test can't answer?"

His face flushed red. "You think you're
pregnant?"

She socked his arm. "Why didn't you ever
tell me you never got your vasectomy? I
haven't been using birth control!"

With elusive typical male logic, he shrugged
like a kid who'd forgotten to bring his home-
work to class.

Jaynie dashed across the room. "I'll be right
back." She swept into the bathroom, closing the
door behind her.

Fishing through the back of the sink cabinet,
she searched for two of the three pregnancy tests
she had purchased when she'd signed on at the
cryobank. She'd become pregnant after the very
first insemination and had never needed the
other two. Finding the packages, she checked
the expiration date. It was still good. Carefully
following the instruction insert, she set to work.

A minute later she heard tapping. "Hey, I want in on this, too," Terrance said from the other side.

She'd kept her eyes closed, waiting the required two minutes to read the response. Now, opening both her eyes, and the door, she welcomed her eager-beaver husband inside. A massive look of expectation covered his face.

She studied the applicator strip lying flat on the counter. Pointing to the result window displaying a blue "plus" sign, Jaynie reeled with instant knowledge.

Terrance raised his shoulders and eyebrows, waiting for the verdict. "Well?"

"Well, considering you never got the vasectomy, the only question is, why did it take this long?" She showed him the pregnancy test wand. "I'm pregnant!"

She leapt into his open arms and wrapped her legs around his waist. He held her firmly and spun around with joy. "Woohoo!"

"This is astounding—just astounding," he kept saying.

They stopped spinning long enough to kiss. His mouth clamped down on hers until they clanked teeth. Jaynie kissed him as if she hadn't seen him in years, anchoring his head with both of her hands and planting her lips over his again and again. One large hand held her hips in place while the other roamed her back. He eased her to sit on the bathroom counter so he could be attentive with both of his hands, and delved in for another world-class kiss.

After a few moments, they settled into softer kisses, warmed with love and laughter.

"This time we did it the old-fashioned way," Jaynie said, speaking and grinning over his moist lips.

Terrance consumed her again with a deep, exploring lunge of his tongue, stealing the thoughts right out of her head. He growled and pulled back a smidgen. She felt his hot breath on her lips and cheeks when he spoke.

"The old-fashioned way—yeah, definitely my way of choice."